WHAT WOULD YOU DO IF . . .

you were a neophyte magician who decided to invent a wrathful god for financial gain, then found his all-too-actual wrath aimed directly at you?

you were a champion swimmer forced to swim a crucial race against a... a... a... *mermaid?*

you were caught in the spell of a *guru* whose strange conception of transcendental meditation has you literally falling on your face?

CONSIDER THE POSSIBILITIES!

First time in book form! Seven flights of supreme fancy—by fantasy's reigning monarch

L. SPRAGUE DE CAMP

THE
RELUCTANT
SHAMAN

and Other Fantastic Tales

by
L. SPRAGUE DE CAMP

PYRAMID BOOKS   •   NEW YORK

ACKNOWLEDGMENTS

THE RELUCTANT SHAMAN was first published in *Thrilling Wonder Stories* for April, 1947; copyright 1947 by Standard Magazines, Inc.

THE HARDWOOD PILE was first published in *Street & Smith's Unknown* for September, 1940; copyright 1940 by Street & Smith Publications, Inc. Copyright renewed by L. Sprague de Camp, 1968.

NOTHING IN THE RULES was first published in *Street & Smith's Unknown* for July, 1939; copyright 1939 by Street & Smith Publications, Inc. It was reprinted in *From Unknown Worlds*, N.Y.: Street & Smith Publications, Inc., 1948; London: Atlas Publishing & Distributing Co., Ltd., 1952. Copyright renewed by L. Sprague de Camp, 1966.

THE GHOSTS OF MELVIN PYE was first published in *Thrilling Wonder Stories* for December, 1946; copyright 1946 by Standard Magazines, Inc.

THE WISDOM OF THE EAST was first published in *Unknown Worlds* for August, 1942; copyright 1942 by Street & Smith Publications, Inc.

MR. ARSON was first published in *Unknown Worlds* for December, 1941; copyright 1941 by Street & Smith Publications, Inc. It was reprinted in *The Undesired Princess*, L.A.: Fantasy Publishing Co., Inc., 1951.

KA THE APPALLING was first published in *Fantastic Universe Science Fiction* for August, 1958; copyright 1958 by King-Size Publications, Inc.

THE RELUCTANT SHAMAN AND OTHER FANTASTIC TALES

A PYRAMID BOOK

First printing, November 1970

PYRAMID BOOKS are published by Pyramid Publications
A Division of The Walter Reade Organization, Inc.
444 Madison Avenue, New York, New York 10022, U.S.A.

CONTENTS

THE
RELUCTANT SHAMAN

One fine July day, a tourist took his small boy into a shop in Gahato, New York. The sign over the shop read:

CHIEF SOARING TURTLE
Indian Bead-Work—Pottery

Inside, a stocky, copper-colored man stood amidst a litter of burnt-leather cushions, Navajo blankets made in Connecticut, and similar truck.

"Have you got a small bow-and-arrow outfit?" the tourist asked.

"*Ugh*," said the Indian. He rummaged and produced a small bow and six arrows with rubber knobs for heads.

"Are you a real Indian?" the boy asked.

"*Ugh*. Sure. Heap big chief."

"Where are your feathers?"

"Put away. Only wear um for war-dance."

The tourist paid and started out. At that instant, a copper-colored boy of fifteen years entered from the back.

"Hey, Pop, one of the kittens just et the other!" he called loudly.

The Indian lost his barbaric impassiveness. "What? Jeepers Cripus, what kind of mink farmer do you call yourself? I told you to shift 'em to separate cages yesterday, before they began to fight!"

"I'm sorry, Pop. I guess I forgot."

"You'd better be sorry. That be good money throwed down the sewer."

The tourist's car door slammed, and as the car moved off, the thin voice of the tourist's little boy was wafted back:

"He talks just like anybody else. He don't sound like a real Indian to me."

But Virgil Hathaway, alias Chief Soaring Turtle, was a real Indian. He was a Penobscot from Maine, forty-six years old, a high-school graduate, and—except that he did not bathe as often as some people thought he should—a model citizen.

Shortly after the departure of the tourist, another man came in. This visitor had Hathaway's distinctive muddy coloring and Mongoloid features, though he was fatter, shorter, and older than Hathaway.

"Morning," he said. "You're Virgil Hathaway, ain't-cha?"

"That's who I be, mister."

The man smiled so that his eyes disappeared in fat. "Pleased to know you, Mr. Hathaway. I'm Charlie Catfish, of the Senecas."

"That so? Glad to know you, Mr. Catfish. How about stopping over for some grub?"

"Thanks, but the folks want to make Blue Mountain Lake for lunch. Tell you what you can do. I got eight stone throwers with me. They was let come up here providing they behaved. I got enough to do without dragging them all over, so if you don't mind I'll leave 'em in your charge."

"Stone throwers?" repeated Hathaway blankly.

"You know, *Gahunga*. You can handle 'em even though you're Algonquin, being as you're a descendant of Dekanawida."

"I be what?"

"A descendant of Hiawatha's partner. We keep track—" A horn blast interrupted him. "Sorry, Mr. Hathaway, gotta go. You won't have no trouble." And the fat Indian was gone.

Hathaway was left puzzled and uneasy. It was nice to be descended from Dekanawida, the great Huron chief and cofounder of the Iroquois League. But what were *Gahunga?* His smattering of the Iroquoian dialects included no such term.

Then there was another customer, and after her Harvey Pringle lounged in wearing a sport shirt that showed off his strength and beauty.

"Hi, Virgil," he drawled. "How's every little thing?"

"Pretty good, considering." Hathaway felt a sudden urge to bring his accounts up to date. Young Pringle could waste more time in one hour than most men could in three.

"I finished my ragweed pulling for today."

"Huh?" said Hathaway.

"Yeah. The old man got shirty again about my not doing anything. I said, why take a job away from some poor guy that needs it? So I appointed myself the county's one-man ragweed committee. I pull the stuff up for one hour a day, heh-heh! Babs been in?"

"No," replied Hathaway.

"Oh, well, she knows where to find me." Harvey Pringle yawned and sauntered out. Hathaway wondered what Barbara Scott could see in that useless hulk. Then he listened to the noise.

It was like a quick, faint drumming, queerly muffled, as though the drum were half full of water. Hathaway looked out the screen-door; no parade. Timothy weeds nodded peacefully in the breeze, and from the Moose River came the faint scream of old man Pringle's saw-mill.

The noise seemed to be behind Hathaway, in the shop, like the sound of a small Delco plant in the cellar. The noise increased. It waxed, and eight figures materialized on the rug. They looked like Iroquois warriors two feet tall, complete with moccasins, buckskin leggings, and scalps shaven except for stiff crests on the crown. One squatted and tapped a three-inch drum. The other seven circled around him, occasionally giving the loon cry by slapping the hand against the mouth while uttering a long, shrill yell.

"Hey!" barked Hathaway. The drumming stopped. "Who the devil be you?"

The drummer spoke:

"*Adenlozlakstengen agoiyo—*"

"Whoa! Don't you speak English?"

"Ayuh, mister. I thought if you was a medicine man, you'd talk Iroquois—"

"If I was what?"

"Medicine man. Charlie said he was gonna leave us with one while he went to Canada."

"Be you the stone throwers?"

"Ayuh. I'm chief, name of Gaga, from Cattaraugus County. Anything you want us to do?"

"Yeah. Just disappear for a while." The *Gahunga* disappeared. Hathaway thought that Charlie Catfish had played a dirty trick on him, to spring these aboriginal spooks without explanation.

He brightened when Barbara Scott entered, trim, dark, and energetic. Hathaway approved of energy in other people.

"Have you seen Harvey, Virgil?" she asked. "I had a lunch date with him."

"Uh-huh," said Hathaway. "Prob'ly sleeping on somebody's lawn."

Miss Scott stiffened. "You're as bad as the rest, Virgil. Nobody's fair to poor Harvey."

"Forget it," said Hathaway with a helpless motion of his hands. When a girl toward whom you felt a fatherly affection seemed bent on marrying the worthless son of the town's leading businessman, who was also your landlord, there wasn't much a moderate man could do. "You still be having that séance tomorrow night?"

"Yep. Dan Pringle's coming."

"*What?* He swears you're a fake."

"I know, but maybe I can win him over."

"Look here, Babs, why does a nice girl like you do all this phony spook business?"

"Money, that's why. Being a secretary and notary won't get me through my last year of college. As for being phony, how about that ug-wug dialect you use on the tourists?"

"That be different."

"Oh, that be different, be it? Here's Harvey now; so long."

The eight *Gahunga* reappeared.

"What you want us to do for you, mister?" asked Gaga. "Charlie told us to be helpful, and by *Iuskeha,* we're gonna be."

"Don't exactly know," Hathaway cautiously replied.

"Is there anything you want?"

"Well," said Hathaway, "I got a good breeding female mink I wish somebody'd offer me five hundred bucks for."

The *Gahunga* muttered together.

"I'm afraid we can't do anything about that," Gaga said finally. "Anything else?"

"Well, I wish more customers would come in to buy my Indian junk."

"Whoopee! U-u-u-u!" shrilled Gaga, drumming. "Come on!"

The seven pranced and stamped for a few seconds, then vanished. Hathaway uneasily waited on a customer, wondering what the *Gahunga* were up to.

Earl Delacroix, owner of The Pines Tea-Shoppe, was passing on the other side of the street, when he leaped and yelled. He came down rubbing his shoulder and looking about resentfully. As soon as he started to walk, there was a flat *spat* of a high-speed pebble striking his clothes, and he jumped again. *Spat! Spat!* The bombardment continued until he hurled himself into Chief Soaring Turtle's shop.

"Somebody's shooting me with an air rifle!" he gasped.

"Bad business," agreed Hàthaway.

There was another yell, and Hathaway looked out. Leon Buttolf was being driven inexorably down the street to the shop. As soon as he was inside, the bombardment overtook Mrs. Camaret, wife of a worker in Pringle's mill.

By the time she had been herded in, the streets were deserted.

"Somebody ought to go to jail for this," Buttolf said.

"That's right," said Delacroix. He looked keenly at Hathaway. "Wonder how everybody gets chased in here?"

"If I sink you have somesing to do wiz zis, Virgil, I tell my Jean," Mrs. Camaret said. "He come, beat you up, stomp you into a leetle jelly!"

"Jeepers Cripus!" protested Hathaway. "How should I make a BB shot fly out in a circle to hit a man on the far side? And my boy Calvin's out back with the mink. You can go look."

"Aw, we ain't suspecting you," said Buttolf.

"I'll walk with you wherever you be going, and take my chance of getting hit," Hathaway said.

"Fair enough," said Delacroix. So the four went out

and walked down the street a way. Delacroix turned into his restaurant, and the others went about their business. Hathaway hurried back to his shop just as a pebble hit Wallace Downey in the seat of the pants.

"Gaga!" Hathaway yelled in desperation. "Stop it, blast your hide!"

The bombardment ceased. Downey walked off with a look of deep suspicion. When Hathaway entered his shop, the *Gahunga* were sitting on the counter.

Gaga grinned infuriatingly.

"We help you, huh, mister?" he said. "Want some more customers?"

"No!" shouted Hathaway. "I don't want your help. I hope I shan't ever see you again!"

The imps exchanged startled glances. Gaga stood up.

"You don't want to be our boss no more?"

"No! I only want you to leave me alone!"

Gaga drew himself to his full twenty-five inches and folded his arms.

"Okay. We help somebody who appreciates us. Don't like Algonquins anyway." He drummed, and the other seven *Gahunga* did a solemn dance down the counter, disappearing as they came to the pile of miniature birch-bark canoes.

In a few minutes Hathaway's relief was replaced by a faint unease. Perhaps he had been hasty in dismissing the creatures; they had dangerous potentialities.

"Gaga!"

Nothing happened. Calvin Hathaway put in his head.

"Did you call me, Pop?"

"No. Yes I did. Ask your maw when dinner's gonna be ready."

It *had* been a mistake; what would he tell Catfish?

After dinner, Hathaway left his wife in charge of the shop while he went for a walk, to think. In front of

Tate's hardware store he found a noisy group consisting of old man Tate, Wallace Downey, and a state trooper. Tate's window was broken, and he was accusing Downey of breaking it and stealing a fishing rod. Downey accused Tate of throwing the rod at him through the window. Each produced witnesses.

"I was buying some film for my camera in the store when bingo! away goes the winda," a witness said. "Mr. Tate and me, we look around, and we see Wally making off with the rod."

"Did you see Downey inside the window?" asked the trooper.

"No, but it stands to reason—"

"What's your story?" the trooper interrupted him, as he turned inquiringly at Downey.

"I was sitting on the steps of the bank havin' a chaw, when Wally comes along carrying that reel, and *zowie!* out comes the rod through the winda, with busted glass all over the place. If old man Tate didn't throw it at him somebody musta."

Puzzled, the trooper scratched his head. Finally, since Tate had his rod back and the window was insured, he persuaded the two angry men to drop the matter.

"Hello, Virgil," said Downey. "Why does everything screwy have to happen in this town? Say, do you know anything about those BB shot? You yelled something, and they quit."

"I don't know nahthing," said Hathaway innocently. "Some kid with an air rifle, I suppose. What was all this run-in with Tate?"

"I went down to the river to fish," explained Downey. "I had a new tackle, and I no sooner dropped it off the bridge than I got a strike that busted the rod right off short. Musta been the biggest bass in the river. Well, I saved the reel, and I was bringin' it back home when old man Tate shies a new rod at me, right through his window."

Hathaway could see how the *Gahunga* were responsible for these events; they were being "helpful." He left Downey and sauntered down Main Street, passing the Adirondack Association office. Barbara Scott made a face at him through the glass. Hathaway thought she needed to be spanked, either on account of the séances, or her infatuation with Harvey Pringle, or both.

Returning to his shop, the middle-aged Indian noted that the Gahato Garage seemed to have an unusually brisk trade in the repair of tires. The cars included the trooper's Ford with all four tires flat. Bill Bugby and his mechanics were working on tires like maniacs.

The trooper who had handled the Tate-Downey incident was walking about the street, now and then stooping to pick up something. Presently he came back.

"Hey, Bill!" he shouted, and conferred in low tones with Bugby, who presently raised his voice. "You're crazy, Mark!" he cried. "I ain't never done a thing like that in all the years I been here!"

"Maybe so," said the trooper. "But you got to admit that somebody scattered bright new nails all over this street. And if you didn't, who did?"

Hathaway prudently withdrew. He knew who had scattered the nails.

Newcomb, the game warden, lounged into Chief Soaring Turtle's shop and spread his elbows along a counter. Hathaway asked him what he was looking so sad about.

The warden explained.

"I was walking by the bank this afternoon, when a big car drives up and a young man gets out and goes in the bank," he said. "There was a canvas bundle on the back of the car. I didn't think anything of it, only just as I get past it the canvas comes tearing off the bundle, like somebody is pulling it, and there on the bumper is tied a fresh-killed fawn."

"You don't say so?"

"Three months out of season, and no more horns than a pussy-cat. Well, you know and I know there's some of that all the time. I run 'em in when I catch 'em, and if it makes me unpopular that's part of my job. But when this young man comes out and I ask him about it, he admits it—and then it turns out he's Judge Dusenberry's son. Half the village is looking on, so I got to run young Dusenberry in."

"Will that get you into trouble?"

"Don't know; depends on who wins the election next fall. Now, Virgil, I'm not superstitious myself. But some of these people are, especially the Canucks. There's talk of your putting a hoodoo on the town. Some have had rocks thrown at 'em, or something, and Wallace Downey is saying you stopped them. If you can stop it, why can't you start it?"

"I don't know a thing about it," said Hathaway.

"Of course, you don't—I realize that's all nonsense. But I thought you ought to know what folks are saying." And Newcomb slouched out, leaving behind him a much worried Indian.

The next day, Hathaway left his wife in charge of the shop and drove towards Utica. As he was turning on to the state highway, Barbara Scott walked past and called good-morning. He leaned out.

"Hi, Barbara! Be you still going to have your spook hunt?"

"You bet, Chief Wart-on-the-Nose."

"What'll you do if old man Pringle gets up and denounces you as a fake?"

"I don't tell my victims I'm not a fake. I say they can watch and judge for themselves. You don't believe in spirits, do you?"

"Never did. Until a little while ago, that is."

"What the devil do you mean by that crack, Virgil?"

"Oh, just some funny things that happened."

Barbara tactfully refrained from pressing for details.

"I never did either, but lately I've had a feeling I was being followed," she said. "And this morning I found *this* on my dresser." She held out a slip of paper on which was scrawled:

"Don't you worry none about Daniel Pringle that old sower-puss. We will help you against him—G."

"I got an idea who sent this, but it won't do no good to explain now," Hathaway mused. "Only I'd like to see you before your séance. G'by."

Three hours later, Hathaway gave up his search through the stacks of the Utica Public Library, having gone through every volume on anthropology, folklore, and allied subjects. He had learned that the stone throwers belonged to the genus of sprite known to the Iroquois as *Dzhungeun.* They all lived in the southwest part of the state and comprised the stone-throwing *Gahunga,* the fertility-producing *Gendayah,* and the hunting and burrowing *Ohdowa.* But, although it was intimated in several places that the Iroquois shamans had known how to control these spirits, nowhere did it tell how.

Hathaway thought a while. Then he left the library and walked along Genesee Street to a pay telephone. He grunted with pain when he learned the cost of a call to the vicinity of Buffalo, but it couldn't be helped. He resolved, if he ever caught up with Charlie Catfish, to take the money either out of the Seneca's pocket or out of his hide.

"Give me the Tonawanda Reservation," he said.

When he got the reservation, he asked for Charlie Catfish. After a long wait, during which he had to feed the coin box, he was told that Catfish would not be back for weeks.

"Then give me Chief Cornplanter."

Another pause. Then: "He's gone to Buffalo for the day."

"Listen," said Hathaway. "Have you got any medicine men, hexers, spook mediums, or such people among you?"

"Who wants to know?"

"I be Virgil Hathaway, of the Penobscots, member of the Turtle clan and descendant of Dekanawida."

He explained his difficulties. The voice said to wait. Presently an aged voice, speaking badly broken English, came from the receiver.

"Wait, please," said Hathaway. "I got to get me a pencil. My Seneca ain't so hot. . . ."

When Hathaway was driving back to Gahato, he attempted to pass a truck on one of the narrow bridges over the Moose River at McClintock. The truck driver misjudged his clearance, and Hathaway's car stopped with a rending crunch, wedged between the truck and the bridge girders. When the garage people got the vehicles untangled and towed to the garage, Hathaway learned that he faced a four-hour, fifty-dollar repair job before he could start moving again, let alone have his fenders straightened. And the afternoon train north had just left McClintock.

That evening, Barbara Scott had collected the elite of Gahato for her séance: Doc Lenoir and his wife; Levi Macdonald, the bank cashier, and his better half; the Pringles, father and son; and a couple of other persons. Dan Pringle greeted Barbara with a polite but cynical smile. He was plump and wheezed and had seldom been worsted in a deal.

Barbara sat her guests in a circle in semidarkness to

await the arrival of her "influences." When Harvey Pringle
had fallen asleep, she got out her paraphernalia. She sat
on a chair in the cabinet, a thing like a curtained telephone booth, and directed the men to tie her securely to
the chair. Then she told them to drop the curtain and put
out the lights. She warned them not to risk her health by
turning on the lights without authorization. It was not an
absolutely necessary warning, as she could control the
lights herself by a switch inside the cabinet.

On the table between the cabinet and the sitters were
a dinner bell, a trumpet, and a slate. The chair on which
Barbara sat came apart easily. Concealed in the cabinet
was a quantity of absorbent cotton for ectoplasm. There
was also a long-handled grasping device, painted black.
Her own contribution to the techniques of this venerable
racket was a system of small lights which would warn her
if any of the sitters left his chair.

Soon, Barbara gave the right kind of squirm, and the
trick chair came apart. The loose bonds could now be removed. Barbara moaned to cover the sounds of her prep-
arations and chanted a few lines from the *Iliad* in Greek.
She intended to have Socrates as one of her controls this
time.

She was still peeling rope when she was astonished to
hear the dinner bell ring. It wasn't a little *ting* such as
would be made by someone's accidentally touching it, but
a belligerent clangor, such as would be made by a cook
calling mile-away farm hands. The little signal lights
showed all the sitters to be in their seats. The bell rang
this way and that, and the trumpet began to toot.

Barbara Scott had been séancing for several years and
had come to look upon darkness as a friend, but now
childish fears swarmed out of her. The cabinet began to
rock. She screamed. The cabinet rocked more violently.
The door of the false side flew open; the cotton and the
grasper were snatched out. The curtain billowed. The

table began to rock too. From the darkness came an angry roar as the grasper tweaked Doc Lenoir's nose.

From somewhere came the muffled beat of a drum and a long, ululating loon-cry:

"U-u-u-u-u-u-u-u!"

The cabinet tipped over against the table. Barbara fought herself out of the wreckage. She remembered that her private light switch was in series with the room's main switch, so that the lights could not be turned on until the secret switch had been thrown. She felt for it, pushed it, and struggled out of the remains of the cabinet.

The terrified sitters were blinded by the lights and dumb at the spectacle of the medium swathed in loose coils of rope with her hand on the switch, her dress torn, and the beginnings of a black eye. Next they observed that the bell, slate, grasper, and other objects were swooping about the room under their own power.

When the lights came on, there was a yell and a command in an unknown language. The slate smashed down on Dan Pringle's head. While he stood blinking, glasses dangling from one ear and the frame of the slate around his neck, other articles went sailing at him. He stumbled over his overturned chair and bolted for the door. The articles followed.

When Pringle reached the street, pebbles began picking themselves up and throwing themselves after the mill owner. It took about three tries to get his range. Then a pebble no bigger than the end of one's thumb, travelling with air-rifle speed, hit the back of his thigh with a flat *spat*. Pringle yelled, staggered, and kept running. Another glanced off his scalp, drawing blood and making him see stars.

The inhabitants of Gahato were entertained by the unprecedented sight of their leading businessman panting down the main street and turning purple with effort. Every now and then there would be the sound of a pebble striking. Pringle would make a bucking jump and come down running harder than ever.

His eye caught a glimpse of Virgil Hathaway letting himself into his shop, and a faint memory of silly talk about the Indian's supernatural powers stirred his mind. He banked and galloped up the porch steps of Soaring Turtle's establishment just as Hathaway closed the screen door behind him. Pringle went through the door without bothering to reopen it.

"Jeepers Cripus!" exclaimed Hathaway mildly. "What be the matter, Dan?"

"L-l-isten, Virgil! Are you a medicine man?"

"Aw, don't pay no attention to superstitious talk like that—"

"But I gotta have help! They're after me!" And he told all.

"Well!" said Hathaway doubtfully. "I'll see what I can do. But they're Iroquois spooks, and don't think much of us Algonquins. Got some tobacco? All right, pull down the shades."

Hathaway took Pringle's tobacco pouch and opened his shattered screen door. He threw a pinch of tobacco into the dark and chanted in bad Seneca:

> I give you tobacco, Dzhungeun,
> Wanderers of the mountains.
> You hear me and will come.
> I give you tobacco.
> I have done my duty towards you.
> Now you must do yours.
> I have finished speaking.

All eight *Gahunga* imps materialized on the lawn. Hathaway sternly ordered them to come inside. When they were in, he questioned them:

"What have you little twerps been up to now?"

Gaga squirmed. "We was only trying to do Miss Scott a favor," he said. "She wants to put on a good spook show. So we help. She don't like this old punkin Pringle. All right, we throw a scare into him. We wasn't going to hurt him none."

"You know you was let come up here for your vacations only if you didn't use your stone-throwing powers," Hathaway said. "And you know what Eitsinoha does to little imps who don't behave."

"Eitsinoha?" cried Gaga. "You wouldn't tell *her!"*

"Dunno, yet. You deserve it."

"Please, mister, don't say nothing! We won't throw even a sand-grain! I swear by *Iuskeha!* Let us go, and we'll head right back to Cattaraugus!"

Hathaway turned to the quivering Pringle. "Changed your mind about raising my rent, Dan?"

"I'll lower it! Five Dollars!"

"Ten?"

"Seven and a half!"

"Okay. Gaga, you and your boys can disappear. But stick around. And don't do *anything,* understand, unless I tell you to." The *Gahunga* vanished.

Pringle recovered some of his usual self-assurance and said:

"Thanks, Virgil! Don't know what I'd have done without you."

"That's all right, Dan. You better not say anything about this, though. Remember, being a medicine man is a kind of joke among us Indians, like being the High Exalted Potentate of one of those there lodges."

"I understand. So they were doing her a favor, huh? It would be bad enough to have my son marry a phony medium, but I can see where a real one would be worse. No sale, and you can tell her I said so. And Harvey'll do what I say, because he has to in order to eat."

"But—" said Hathaway. He wanted to defend Barbara Scott; to tell Pringle that even if she was a crooked medium in a mild way, she was still better than that no-count son of his.

"What?" said Pringle.

"Nahthing." Hathaway reconsidered; everything was working out fine. Barbara would get over her crush on that big loafer, finish her college, and be able to drop the medium racket. Why stir things up? "Goodnight, Dan."

He hadn't done badly, thought Hathaway as he locked up, considering that he had only been in the medicine-man business a couple of days. He must take a trip out to Tonawanda in the fall and look up Charlie Catfish. Maybe the thing had commercial possibilities.

THE HARDWOOD PILE

This is a world wherein virtue often goes unrewarded. If R. B. Wilcox had not been such a moral man, he might have gotten the true story of the haunted woodpile for his book on the lore and legends of upstate New York. Mr. Wilcox's morals, alone, were not responsible for his failure to get the inside dope. There was also the fact that carroty-red hair did not appeal to him.

The hair belonged to Miss Aceria Jones, the hostess at The Pines. This was a self-styled tea room in the village of Gahato, county of Herkimer, State of New York. The Pines, despite the misleading sobriquet of "tea room," served liquor of all degrees of hardness and had a passable dance orchestra. Not the least of its attractions was Miss Aceria Jones. She was an uncommonly pretty girl, looking rather like a plane hostess.

R. B. Wilcox had landed at The Pines in the course of his prowl around the country after lore and legends. After dinner he tried to collect some material. The restaurateur, a Mr. Earl Delacroix, was out; so the writer tackled Miss Jones. She gave him a little lore on the theory and practice of hostessing in an Adirondack sawmill town, but nothing that could be called a legend. To his questions about the haunted woodpile, she replied that she paid no attention to such silly stories.

In the hope of squeezing a little usable copy out of his charming questionee, Wilcox tried praise: "I'm surprised that you live up here in the sticks. I should think with your looks you could get a job in the city."

"You mean Utica?"

"New York."

"No, I would not like that. No trees."

"You're crazy about trees?"

"Well, some trees. If there was a job in a place with a Norway maple in front of it, I would take it at once."

"A what in front of the place?"

"A Norway maple—*Acer platanoides*. Do you know of a place that has one such?"

"Why . . . uh . . . no. But I don't know much about trees. Is that a native species?"

"No, a European."

"Wouldn't another species do?"

"No; it must be that. I cannot explain. But, Mr. Wilcox, it would mean much to me." She rolled her large eyes meltingly at him.

Wilcox's morals began to assert themselves. He said stiffly: "I'm afraid I don't know what *I* could do for you."

"You could find a nice, clean place that has a job open, and a Norway maple growing in front of it. If you did, I would like you very, *very* much." Another roll of the optics.

At the second "very," Wilcox could fairly feel his morals tugging him toward the door. He, or rather his morals, may have been doing Miss Jones an injustice. But he did not stay to investigate this melancholy redhead's passion for Norway maples, or her definition of "very." He paused only long enough to assure Miss Jones that he would let her know if he heard of anything. Then he passed out of the restaurant and out of this tale.

To get a proper perspective, we must go back to 1824. In that year there landed in New York a dark, paunchy, dignified man who said he was August Rudli of Zurich, Switzerland. He was, he said, a member of an old Swiss banking family, and also related to the Wittelsbachs, so that he was about forty-third in line for the Bavarian throne. He had been a colonel under Napoleon—he had a medal to prove it—and, finding the banking business too stuffy, had taken his share of the family fortune and come to America.

But it must be recorded that Herr Rudli's story contained one or two inexactitudes. He was related neither to the Wittelsbachs nor to any family of bankers. He had seen no military service; the medal was a phony. He had been in the banking business, but not in the way he had said. He had risen by sheer merit to the post of cashier. Thereupon, on a dark and stormy night, he had walked off with all the assets not securely nailed down.

As people were seldom if ever extradited across the Atlantic in those days, at least for embezzlement, Herr Rudli might have enjoyed the fruits of his enterprise for years, if he had not fallen in with an even slicker article. This article, one John A. Spooner, separated Rudli from most of his cash for a "country estate" consisting of several thousand acres of granite ridges, bog holes, and black flies in the Adirondacks. Rudli spent most of the rest in having a road run in, a biggish house built, and gewgaws imported from Europe to furnish the house. Among the more puzzling importations were two young Norway maples, which were planted in front of the house. Rudli's tract was already covered by a dense mixed forest consisting partly of sugar maple, red maple and silver maple, the first of which grow at least as large and as fast as any European maple. But Rudli had his own ideas about being a country gentleman, and the planting of imported trees evidently formed part of them.

Rudli never learned how thoroughly he had been roodled. He died of pneumonia in the middle of the first winter he attempted to spend in his new house.

After Rudli's death, the tract went through various hands. Some of it ended up as the property of the International Paper Co.; some went to the State of New York; the piece on which Rudli's house had stood went to a man named Delahanty. After a century of neglect, all that could be seen of the house was a broad, low mound covered with leaf mold, from which one stone chimney stuck up. The clearing in which the house had stood and most of the road leading to it were completely grown up. Of the two Norway maples, one had died in infancy. The other was now a fine, big tree.

Delahanty the elder sold his pulpwood stumpage in 1903. Thirty-five years later, Delahanty the younger sold the hardwood on the tract. In went the lumberjacks through the snow, and down came the beeches, birches, and hard maples. Down, too, came Rudli's surviving Norway maple, mistaken for a sugar maple, the "hard" maple of the lumberman.

In due course, the two logs that had been cut from this tree arrived in the hot pond of Dan Pringle's sawmill at Gahato. The name of the village is Mohawk for "log-in-the-water"; very appropriate for a sawmill town. In the spring, they were hauled up the jacker chain and sawn into about nine hundred feet of one-inch boards. These were put in Pile No. 1027, which consisted of one-inch FAS hard maple. FAS—Firsts and Seconds—is the highest hardwood classification.

The following summer, Pringle got a hardwood order from Hoyt, his wholesaler, that included twenty thousand feet of one-inch FAS hard maple. The yard crew loaded the top halves of Piles No. 1027 and 1040 into a box car. The foreman, Joe Larochelle, ordered them to transfer the remaining half of Pile 1027 to Pile 1040. So Henri Michod lowered himself from the hardwood tramway to the top of Pile No. 1027. He picked up a board and handed it to Olaf Bergen, who turned and plunked it on a lumber truck, which stood on the tramway with its wheels chocked. Bergen took his pipe out long enough to spit—aiming between the tramway and the pile— steered the pipe back through the mossy curtain of yellow hair that hung from his upper lip, grabbed the next board, and so forth. When Michod had finished the topmost course of boards, he gathered up the stickers—the one-by-two's that keep the courses apart—piled them on the tramway, and went on to the next course.

That was all very well. But when Michod started on the fourth course, the pile began to sway. First it swayed east and west, then north and south, then with a circular motion. It also set up a dismal moaning and squeaking as board and stickers rubbed together.

Olaf Bergen stared in childish wonder at the phenomenon. "Hey, Henri, what the Holy Jumping Judas you doing with that pile?"

"Me?" cried the harassed Michod. "I don't do nothing. It does it. Earthquake, maybe. I think I get the hell off." He jumped off the pile on a lower one with a clatter.

"Can't be no earthquake," Bergen called down to him. "You don't see the other piles actin' up, do you?"

"No."

"Well, if it was an earthquake, the other piles would have swayed, too, wouldn't they? So there wasn't no earthquake. Stands to reason, don't it?"

"Yeah? Then what makes the pile sway?"

"Nothin'. An earthquake's the only thing that could, and there wasn't no earthquake. So the pile didn't sway. Now get back up and gimme some more boards."

"So the pile didn't sway, huh? *Les nuts,* Mr. Bergen. I know better. And, by damn, I don't get back up there."

"Aw, come on, Henri. Stands to reason it must have been your imagination."

"All right, you stand on the pile then. I take the tramway." Michod swarmed up onto the trestle. Bergen, looking confident, jumped down onto No. 1027.

But No. 1027 had its own ideas, if lumber piles can be said to have ideas. The pile began to sway again. Bergen, staggering to keep his balance, perforce had to sway, too. And with each sway his china-blue eyes got bigger.

The motion was not a very unpleasant or difficult one; in fact, it was rather like that of the deck of a ship in a stiff breeze. But that did not calm Olaf Bergen. The trouble was that this lumber pile was not the deck of a ship. Lumber piles do not, normally, act that way. A pile that does so is unnatural, perhaps unholy. Olaf Bergen wanted no part of such a pile; not even a splinter.

So he shrieked: "The damn thing's haunted!" and tumbled off even more quickly than Michod had done. There was a brief swishing of his work shoes through the weeds, and the lumber yards knew him no more, at least not that day.

Henri Michod sat down on the tramway and took out a pack of cigarettes. He would have to report this singular occurrence to Joe Larochelle, but that was no reason for not relaxing a little first.

Then he heard Larochelle's quick footsteps coming down the tramway and put away his cigarettes. Nobody walked quite so fast as Larochelle. He always arrived places slightly out of breath, and when he talked his sentences fell over one another. By these means he created an illusion of being an intensely busy man, passionately devoted to his employer's interests. Medium-sized, baldish, and snaggle-toothed, he trotted up and gasped: "Wh-where . . . where's Ole?"

"Ole?" replied Michod. "He's gone home."

"You mean to say that lousy guy went home without saying anything to me and here I've got three cars of grain-door board to get loaded in time for the noon freight?"

"That's it, Joe."

"Was he sick?"

"Maybe. He got kind of upset when this pile began to sway under him."

"Well, of all the lousy tricks! You wait here; I'll send Jean Camaret over from the pine tram. What the hell kind of a place does he think this is, anyhow?"—and Larochelle was off again.

Presently Jean Camaret appeared. He was older and even beefier than Henri Michod, who was pretty beefy himself. Between themselves they spoke Canuck French, which is not quite the same as French French. More than one Frenchman has indignantly denied that it is French at all.

Camaret got on Pile No. 1027. Before he had time to do more, the pile began to sway again. Camaret looked up. "Is it that I am dizzy, or is it that this sacred pile shakes herself?"

"The pile shakes herself, I think. It is a thing most extraordinary. It is not the wind, and it is not the earthquake. But it makes nothing. Give me a board just the same."

Camaret was, through no desire of his own, giving a first-rate imitation of a reed in a gale, but anyone could see that his heart was not in the part. He was not suited to it. There was nothing reedlike about him. He spread his

feet to brace himself, made a fumbling effort to pick up a
board, then turned a large, red, joyless face up to Michod.

"I cannot move," he said. "This unhappy pile gives
me the sickness of the sea. Aid me to mount, my old."

His old helped him on the tramway. He sat down, put
his head in his hands, and groaned like a soul in purga-
tory.

Michod grinned unsympathetically. At this rate, he
would get a day's pay for doing no work at all. He started
to take out his cigarettes again, but Joe Larochelle bustled
down the tramway. "Wh-what . . . what's the matter with
Jean? Is he sick or something?"

Camaret groaned again, more horribly. "I have the
sick to the stomach. The pile goes *comme ci—comme ça.*"

"Whaddya mean the pile goes this way and that way?
What the hell's the matter with you? Scared because a
pile sways a little?"

"This pile is different. You get on and see."

"Huh! Never thought I'd see a grown man like you
scared of a little pile. What the hell, I'm not scared—"
And Larochelle hopped off the tramway. The pile began
its rocking-chair act. Larochelle yelped and scrambled
back on the trestle.

"Anybody can see that pile ain't safe!" he bawled.
"Must be the foundation beams are gone all to hell. Why
the hell didn't you tell me sooner, Henri? Want us to break
our necks?"

Henri Michod knew better than to argue. He grinned
cynically and shrugged.

Larochelle concluded: "Well, anyway, you guys go over
and help on the pine tram. Come back here at one."

When Camaret and Michod returned to Pile No. 1027
after the noon hour, they saw that Larochelle had tied it
to the neighboring piles with a half-inch rope. He explained: "The foundation beams are okay; I don't see

what the hell's wrong unless the supports are high in the middle so she's—whatcha call it?—unstable. But she ought to hold still with all this guying."

Neither yard worker showed any enthusiasm for getting back on the pile. Finally Larochelle shouted: "Damn it, Henri, you get on that pile or I'll put you on the soda tank!"

So Michod got, albeit sullenly. Larochelle referred to the tank of preserving solution in which freshly sawn pine planks were dunked. In pulling boards out of this tank, one had to move quickly to keep the next board from hitting one, and the solution made one's hands crack after a day. Larochelle's favorite method of settling arguments was to threaten to put a man on the disagreeable tank job out of his regular turn.

They loaded the truck, pushed it down to Pile No. 1040, and unloaded it. When this had been done twice, Larochelle put another man on the job, to stand on the edge of the pile and pass boards up. No. 1027 groaned and creaked a good deal, but the guying kept it from doing its hula.

The new man, Edward Gallivan, picked up a board and handed it to Michod, who passed it up to Camaret. Gallivan had picked up another board, when the first board twisted itself out of Camaret's hands. It flew back down, landing on Gallivan's board. Thus Camaret found himself boardless, while Gallivan had two boards.

Now Edward Gallivan liked mill-yard work well enough, but not to the point of collecting hard-maple planks for the fun of it. He cried:

"Hey, Frenchy, watch what you're doin'! You damn near took the head off me with that thing."

Camaret muttered something apologetic and looked puzzled. Michod passed the errant board up again. Again it twisted itself away from Camaret and returned to the pile with a clatter.

Camaret looked down with an expression of perplexity, suspicion, reproach, and growing alarm. That is, he would have looked that way if the human face were capable of expressing so many emotions at once. "Henri," he said, "did you grab that board away from me?"

"Why would I go grabbing boards away from you? I got enough boards already."

"I don't ask that. Did you snatch her?"

"No, by damn, I didn't. I ain't no board-snatcher."

"Now, boys," said Gallivan, "we ain't getting nowheres arguin' like this. You do it over and I'll watch."

So Michod passed the board up a third time. When Camaret took it, it swung wildly and twisted like a live thing. Camaret released it to keep from being pulled off the tramway, and it floated gently back to the place from which Gallivan had picked it. "Saints preserve us!" cried Gallivan. "I don't like that."

Michod folded his arms triumphantly. "You satisfied, Jean? I didn't have nothing to do with that."

Camaret replied hollowly: "Me, I am satisfied. I am satisfied too much. I get the sick to the stomach when I think of that. You tell Joe I go. I go home, get drunk, beat my wife, forget all about these damn boards."

Joe Larochelle blew up when the state of affairs was explained to him. Ned Gallivan smiled paternally, and Henri Michod shrugged. Larochelle had recently turned in a certain credit slip for eight hundred feet of No. 1 Common Birch, of which the local customer had not returned all the allegedly unused lumber. Maybe it was a bona fide mistake; maybe Larochelle had not split the proceeds of the discrepancy with the customer. But Gallivan and Michod knew about the slip and were pretty sure of their own positions in consequence.

Finally Larochelle yelled: "All right, all right! I'll show you how to handle these jumping boards. You wait here—" When he returned he carried a double-bitted ax. "Now," he said, "Henri, you hand a board to Ned."

When Gallivan took the board, it apparently tried to pull him off the trestle. Larochelle, standing beside him, smacked the board with the flat of the ax. It quivered a bit and subsided.

"Ouch!" said Gallivan. "You're making my hands sting."

"Never mind that, it's the way to handle 'em. I'm the guy who has to figure everything out—" Larochelle's expedient seemed to have cowed the boards, temporarily at least. They went up without protest.

Michod thought, that was just like the stupid, pretending that nothing was wrong. Anybody could see that here was something of the most extraordinary. That was the way of the world. The stupids like Larochelle had the authority, while the intelligents like himself—

This reverie was interrupted by another singular occurrence. Michod carelessly shot a board up to Gallivan when the latter was busy fishing his eating-tobacco out of his pants pocket. Gallivan made a one-handed grab and missed. It did not much matter, for the board kept right on going. It described a graceful arc and settled cozily into its appointed place on the truck.

"Hey!" yelled Larochelle. "Don't go throwing those boards; you're liable to hit somebody."

Michod kept silent, not wanting to disillusion the others about his strength and adroitness. Gallivan caught the next board; it hoisted him a foot into the air before he stopped it.

"What the hell are you trying to do, Henri?" cried the surprised Gallivan.

It was all very well to get credit for the mill-yard equivalent of tossing the caber, but to be blamed for all the vagaries of these athletic boards was something else. So Michod spoke up:

"I'm not trying to do nothing, by damn. I—" He was interrupted by finding his hands unexpectedly full of board. But the board did not stay there. It ripped his mittens in its eagerness to get up into Gallivan's hands, and thence on the truck.

Larochelle shrieked: "Stop it! Stop them!" As well try to stop a nestful of hornets by reading Jean Jacques Rousseau to them. All over the pile, boards were bouncing into Michod's uneager grasp, then flinging themselves up to Gallivan and on the truck. The load grew by leaps and even a bound or two. When they stopped, the truck was piled dangerously high. The last board took time out to thwack Joe Larochelle in passing. The foreman toppled from the tramway. As he did so he grabbed Gallivan for support. Both landed on the unfortunate Michod with a great clatter.

They picked themselves up to see the truck moving down the track of its own accord. Larochelle, who among his very modest list of virtues certainly counted energy, scrambled back onto the tramway in pursuit. The truck stopped in front of No. 1040, and its load cascaded crashingly off.

"Hey, look down!" said Michod.

The three men got down on their knees and peered over the edge of the trestle. A board had fallen off the truck during its trip and gone down between the tramway and the piles. It was now crawling after the fashion of an inchworm through the weeds. Arriving at No. 1040, it began to hump itself up the pile's side. Now and then it would be jerked upward without visible effort on its part. Its motions were like those of a rather obtuse puppy whose owner is trying to teach it tricks and putting it through them by *force majeure* when it fails to get the idea. Finally, it left the step-boards on the side of the pile and swooped up on the disorderly tangle on top of No. 1040.

Joe Larochelle did not acknowledge defeat easily. No matter how red-handed one caught him in a bit of grafting, he was as firm as an early Christian martyr and as plausible as a street map in his denials. But now he said:

"It's too much for me. You boys can go home; I gotta see the boss."

Joe Larochelle repaired to Pringle's office, which was downstairs in his home. He told his story.

Dan Pringle was a small, plump man with a large watch chain decorated with an incisor tooth of *Cervus canadensis* —the wapiti. He asked: "You been drinking lately, Joe?"

"No, Mr. Pringle. I ain't touched a thing."

Pringle got up and sniffed. "Well, I guess maybe not. Do you suppose a union organizer was back of this?"

"No, there ain't been any around. I been watching for them."

"Did you look between the piles and under the tram-ways?"

"Sure, I looked everywhere."

"Well, maybe. They're apt to sneak in no matter how careful you are, you know. Suppose you come back after supper and we'll take a look at these fancy boards. And bring a flashlight. We'll look around for union organizers, just in case."

Pringle and Larochelle arrived at the lumber yard as the sun was sliding down behind Gahato Mountain. Pringle insisted on creeping around the piles with his flash-light as if he were playing gangsters and G-men. He was, he explained, hoping to surprise a lurking union organizer. At Pile No. 1040 Larochelle said:

"That's her. See them boards lying in a heap on top?"

Pringle saw the boards. He also saw a young woman sitting on the edge of the pile, swinging her sandaled feet. Her green dress had obviously seen better days. About her hair, the kindest comment would be that it looked "non-chalant" or "carefree." It had apparently been red, but it had been singed off. It had grown out again but was still black at the ends and presented a distressing aspect.

"Good evening," said the young woman. "You are Mr. Pringle, the owner of the sawmill, are you not?"

"Why—uh—maybe," said Pringle suspiciously. "Who — I mean what can I do for you?"

"Huh?" said a puzzled voice at his side. "What do you mean, Mr. Pringle?" Joe Larochelle was looking at him, ignoring the girl, whose feet were a few feet away on a level with his face.

"Why—I was talking—".

"You *are* the owner, Mr. Pringle? I have heard the men talking about you," said the girl.

"Just thinking out loud?" said Larochelle.

"Yes— I mean maybe," said the confused Pringle. "She just asked me—"

"Who's 'she'?" asked Larochelle.

"That young lady."

"What young lady?"

Pringle decided that his foreman was simply dithering and asked the girl: "You're not a union organizer, are you?"

The girl and Larochelle answered simultaneously: "I don't know what that is. I don't think so." "Who, *me?* Aw, come on, Mr. Pringle, you oughta know I hate 'em as much as you—"

"Not you, Joe!" cried Pringle. "Not you! I was just asking her—"

Larochelle's patience began to wear thin. "And I been asking you who 'her' is?"

"How should I know? I've been trying to find out myself."

"I think we're kinda mixed up. Here you talk about some skirt and I ask who and you say you don't know. That don't make sense, does it?"

Pringle wiped his forehead.

The girl said: "I would like to see you, Mr. Pringle, only without this M'sieu' Larochelle."

"We'll see, miss," said Pringle.

Larochelle spoke: "Say, Mr. Pringle, are you feeling well? Damned if you don't sound like you was talking to somebody who ain't there."

Pringle began to feel like a rat in the hands of an experimental psychologist who is, with the best of motives, trying to drive it crazy. "Don't be ridiculous, Joe. I sound as though I were talking to somebody who *is* there."

"I know; that's just the trouble."

"What's the trouble?"

"There *ain't* anybody there, of course!"

This statement, despite its alarming implications, gave Pringle a feeling of relief. Theretofore, this maddening dispute had been like fighting blindfolded with broadswords at sixty paces. Now he had a solid point of disagreement. He said sharply: "Are you sure *you're* feeling well, Joe?"

"Sure, of course, I'm well."

"Do you, or don't you, see a girl in a green dress sitting on the edge of the pile?"

"No. I just said there ain't anybody there."

"Didn't ask you whether anybody *was* there, but whether you *saw* anybody there."

"Well, if there was anybody there I'd see 'em, wouldn't I? Makes sense, don't it?"

"We'll waive that."

"Wave what? This green dress I'm supposed to see that ain't there?"

Pringle danced distractedly on his short legs. "Never mind, never mind! Have you heard a woman's voice coming from that pile?"

"No, of course not. What gives you the idea—"

"All right, all right, that's what I wanted to know. You can run along home now. I'll do the rest of the investigating myself. No"—as Larochelle started to protest—"I mean that."

"Oh, all right. But look out the union organizers don't get you."

Larochelle grinned maliciously and trotted off. Pringle winced visibly at the last words but bravely faced the pile.

"Now, young lady," he said grimly, "are you *sure* you're not a union organizer?"

"Would I know if I was, Mr. Pringle?"

"You bet you would. I guess you aren't one, maybe. More likely an hallucination."

"Mr. Pringle! I did not ask to see you so you could call me bad names."

"No offense meant. But something's very funny around here. Either Joe or I are seeing things."

"If you have good eyes, you always see things. What is wrong with that?"

"Nothing, when the things are there. What I'm trying to find out is, are you real or am I imagining you?"

"You see me, no?"

"Sure. But that doesn't prove you're real."

"What do I do to prove I am real?"

"I'm not just sure myself. You could put out your hand," he said doubtfully. The girl reached down, and Pringle touched her hand. "Feels real enough. But maybe I'm imagining the feel. How come Joe didn't see you?"

"I did not want him to."

"Oh, just like that, eh? You don't want him to, so he looks right through you."

"Naturally."

"It may be natural to you. But when I look at somebody I generally see him. Let's forget that question for a while. Let's not even think about it. If I'm not nuts already, I will be soon at this rate. Just what is all this funny business?"

"I don't think it is funny to have my home broken up."

"Huh?"

"You broke up my home."

"I broke up your home. I broke up your home. Young lady— What's your name, by the way?"

"Aceria."

"Miss Aceria, or Aceria something?"

"Just Aceria."

"Oh, well, skip it. I used to consider myself a pretty intelligent man. Not any parlor-pink intellectual, you understand, but a good, competent American businessman. But I'm not sure any more. Nothing seems to make sense. What in the name of the great horn spoon do you mean, I've broken up your home? Did I lead your husband astray, maybe?"

"Oh, not like that. Like *that!*" She pointed to the tangle of boards behind her. "That was my home."

"Those boards? Come on, don't try to tell me some man of mine tore your house down and sneaked the boards onto the pile."

"Well, yes and no. Those boards were my tree."

"Your *what?*"

"My tree. I lived in it."

"I suppose you'll say next you were responsible for that commotion today?"

"I am afraid yes."

"Well." Others had testified to the occurrence of the commotion. Or had Pringle imagined that Joe Larochelle had told that story— No, no, no! He wasn't going to think about that any more. "What was the idea?"

"I wanted to keep my home together. First I tried to keep the men from moving the boards. When I could not, I hurried the last ones up to get them together again."

"What *are* you? Some kind of spook?"

"I am a sphendamniad. That is a kind of wood nymph. Some people would say dryad, but that is not just right. They are oak spirits. I am a maple spirit. A man brought my tree from Austria, more than a hundred years ago. Last winter your men cut my tree down. I could not stop them, because I was hibernating, I think you call it, and by the time I woke up it was too late. That is how my hair got burned, when the men burned the branches and tops. It has grown out, but I know it looks terrible. I cannot leave my home on weekdays to go to the hairdresser, for fear the men will move the boards."

"You mean those aren't real hard maple?" snapped Pringle with sudden alertness. He climbed the side of the pile with an agility remarkable in a man of his age and girth. He looked at the boards with his flashlight. "Yeah, the grain *isn't* quite the same. Let's see; if they fooled the grader . . . I guess maybe they can go out with the rest on Tuesday."

"You mean you are going to sell these boards?"

"Sure. Just got a big order from Hoyt."

"What will happen to them?"

"Dunno. They'll be made into desks and bureau drawers and things, maybe. Depends on who buys them from Hoyt."

"But you must not do that, Mr. Pringle! My home, it will be scattered. I will have no place to live."

"Can't you set up housekeeping in another tree?"

"I can only live in Norway maples, and there are no more around here."

"Well, do you want to buy them? I'll let you have them at eighty dollars a thousand, which is less than I could get in the open market."

"I have no money."

"Well then, they'll have to go out with the rest. Sorry if it inconveniences you, but the sawmill costs alone are over seven dollars a thousand, counting insurance and depreciation."

"I do not know about such things, Mr. Pringle. I know you will break up my home so I can never get it together again. You would not do that, yes? I would like you *so* much if you did not."

She looked appealingly at him, a tear trickling down one cheek. If she had done this earlier, while it was still light, it might have worked. But all Pringle could see of her face was a dim, pale oval in the darkness; so he snapped:

"You bet I'd do that! This is business, young lady. If I let sentiment interfere with business, I'd have gone broke long ago. Anyway, I'm not convinced that you exist. So why should I give away lumber I paid good money for to somebody who's a mere hallucination, maybe?"

"You are a bad, wicked man. I will never let you send these boards away."

"Oh," he grinned through the dark. "It's to be a fight, huh? Nobody ever accused Dan Pringle of running away from a good, honest business fight. We'll see. Good night, Miss Aceria."

Pringle was as good as his word. Monday morning, he called in Larochelle and told him to load the lumber in Pile No. 1040 that day, instead of Tuesday as planned.

Michod, Camaret, Gallivan, and Bergen all looked solemn when they saw they were to work on No. 1040. But Larochelle forestalled any objections by mention of the soda tank.

So they set up the rollers. These were objects that looked like iron ladders, except that on what would be the rungs were mounted steel sleeves rotating on ball bearings. The rollers were mounted end to end on sawhorses so that they could carry boards across the tramway and across the tops of the two low piles between the tramway and the railroad spur.

Fassler, the inspector, turned the first board over with the sharpened T-piece on the end of his flexible lumber rule and made a note on his tally sheet. Gallivan, wondering if he hadn't been several kinds of fool for taking the job on Pile No. 1040, picked up the board and gave it to Michod. Michod put it on the nearest roller and shoved. *Zing!* went the rolls and away went the board.

In the normal course of events, the board should have continued its way to the box car, where Camaret and Bergen awaited it. Their mittens were outstretched to seize it, when it slowed down, stopped, and reversed its motion. *Zing!* went the rolls, but this time in reverse. Michod stared at it dumbly as it shot past under his nose, left the end of the line of rollers, and slammed down on the top of the pile.

Aceria had not been caught napping.

But Fassler knew nothing about Aceria, except for some vague talk, which he had discounted, about jumping boards. Since the tramway was between him and the box car, he could not see what had happened and assumed that somebody had pushed the board back up the rollers. He said so, with embellishments. He was a very profane man, though a slight, stoop-shouldered, harmless-looking one. People liked to play jokes on him so that they could stand around and admire his profanity.

Gallivan grinned at him. "Hey, Archie, will you say some more? Sure, it's as good as an education for a man to listen to you."

But the others were not so amused. Camaret and Bergen came up from the car. Camaret said: "I begin to get the sick to the stomach again."

Bergen said: "I'm damned if I'll work in a yard that's full of spooks."

Michod cocked a skeptical eyebrow. "You don't believe in those things, Ole?"

"Well, not exactly. But there's a powerful lot of queer things you don't know about."

"All right. You argue. I take a rest." And Michod sat down to enjoy a smoke.

The others explained to the incredulous Fassler. Finally, not knowing what else to do, they went back to work. Michod undertook to conduct the next board personally down to the box car. It went along reluctantly; just before they arrived, it shot forward, in one door of the car and out the other into the weeds before Camaret and Bergen could stop it.

So Joe Larochelle presently found his workers sitting on the tramway and settling the affairs of the universe. He yelled:

"You get back there and load that stuff or, by jeepers, you can start looking for another job!"

Gallivan grinned. "Sure, now, wouldn't that be a terrible thing?" He lowered his voice. "And wouldn't it be terrible, Joe, if the boss found out about that credit slip you turned in for Jack Smeed?"

"I dunno what you're talking about," said Larochelle. "But, anyway, I guess there's some other stuff you can pile."

So nothing more was done to Pile No. 1040 that day. Larochelle, if he had a soul, wrestled with it mightily. He had definite orders from Pringle, but he could not adopt the usual method of enforcing them because of the delicate credit-slip situation. By Tuesday night he worked up enough courage to report to Pringle.

Pringle snapped: "Sounds like they're getting pretty damned independent. Maybe a union organizer got next to them, after all. Let's see. I'll think of something by tomorrow, maybe."

Neither was altogether candid. Larochelle obviously could not explain why he could not get tougher with the yard crew, and Pringle could not explain about Aceria for fear of having people tap their foreheads. He was not too sure about his sanity himself. He thought of going down the line to Utica to be looked over, but he was

afraid to do that for fear the doctor *would* find something
wrong with his clockwork.

Wednesday morning, Pringle wandered down to the
sawmill. There he saw something that filled him with dis-
may and apprehension. It was nothing more than an
elderly, dried-up man looking at a box car standing on the
end of the spur. That seems like a harmless enough com-
bination. But the elderly man was the New York Central
freight agent, and the car was one that had arrived with
a carload of lime some months before. Pringle had not
had any place to store the lime, had not wanted to build
a shed, and had not wanted to pay demurrage on the car.
So he had had the car jacked down to the end of the spur
and hidden with brush. There it had stood, serving as free
storage space while Pringle unloaded at his leisure and
the Central wondered vaguely what had become of their
car. Now the camouflage had been removed.

"We been wondering where that car was," accused
Adams, the agent.

"I guess maybe it just slipped my mind," replied Pringle
lamely.

"Mebbe. Looks like you owe us about three months'
demurrage. I'll get the bill out first thing tomorra." And
Adams walked off uncompromisingly.

Later, Pringle grated to Larochelle: "If I find who took
that brush away, I'll kill the—"

When Larochelle departed, a woman's voice said: "I
took the branches away from the car, Mr. Pringle." There
she was, standing between a couple of piles.

"You—" sputtered Pringle. He got a grip on himself.
"I suppose maybe you think you're smart, young lady?"

"Oh, but I *know* I am smart," she replied innocently.
"I thought out that you wanted the car hidden all by myself."

"Well, if you think it's going to make any difference

about those boards, you can change your idea. They're going in spite of hell or high water."

"Yes? We will see, as you said that night." And she vanished.

Pringle yelled after Larochelle: "Hey, Joe! Spot a car for No. 1040 right away. If the hardwood gang don't want to work on it, get some men from the pine gang." He muttered to himself: "I'll show this wood spook! Thinks she can scare me—"

But the men from the pine gang fared no better than the hardwood gang. They fared rather worse, in fact. The boards slewed crosswise on the rollers, jumped off the pile, paddled the men, and finally hit one man, Dennis Ahearn, over the head. He required two stitches in his scalp, and there were no more attempts to load the car that day.

As Ahearn himself explained: "It may be the spooks, or it may be the wood, or it may be the sap runnin', but the divil himself won't get me to touch another of them damn live boards. What you need, Mr. Pringle, is a crew of lion tamers."

Pringle was angry enough over his failure to get the car loaded. But he was a shrewd man; he would not have lasted so long as he had in the precarious Adirondack lumber business otherwise. He suspected that Aceria would try some devilment or other in retaliation for his latest attempt to load the car. Maybe there would be an accident in the mill—so he ordered extra guard rails installed around the saws. Or, he thought, he might find some morning that all the lumber trucks were at the bottom of the Moose River. True, they weighed over three hundred pounds apiece, but he was not taking any chances with Aceria's supernatural powers, whatever they were. So he hired some of the workers overtime as night watchmen.

But Aceria was not exactly stupid either. Uninformed, perhaps, as a result of living in the woods for so many centuries, but she learned quickly. So her next attack was in a quarter that Pringle had not thought of.

Mrs. Pringle, a waspish woman, was due back at Pringle's home from a visit to some relatives. There was not much pleasurable anticipation of the reunion on either side. The corrosive effect of Helen Pringle's disposition, applied over a period of thirty years, had seen to that. But whatever Helen Pringle expected, she did not expect to find a comely young woman sitting at *her* dressing table, in *her* bedroom, calmly drying a head of freshly shampooed carroty-red hair.

Aceria looked up with a quick smile at Mrs. Pringle's gasp. "Yes?" she said politely.

Mrs. Pringle's mouth moved soundlessly. Then she said: "Gug."

"I'm sorry."

"You . . . you . . . what . . . what are you doing in my room?"

It was the first time since she had been five years old that words had failed—or almost failed—Mrs. Pringle. But then, the fact that Aceria was not wearing her green dress might have had something to do with it.

Aceria, still polite, remarked: "Your room? Oh, *I* see, you are Mrs. Pringle! This is embarrassing. It was stupid of Danny not to send me away before you came back, no? But if you will leave me for a minute, I will be gone like a flash."

Thus it came to pass that Pringle found the reunion more exciting, if no more pleasant, than he had expected. Helen descended on him and demanded to know, in a voice like a band saw going through a twenty-four-inch pine log—with knots in it—who that creature was, and didn't he have sense enough to know that nobody would want an old fool like him for anything but his money, and if he had to make a fool of himself couldn't he have the decency to keep his follies out of his wife's sight, and it was a good thing she hadn't unpacked because she was leaving forthwith. Which she did.

Through this tirade, Pringle was merely bewildered until the end. As Helen slammed the door behind her he saw the light and dashed upstairs. There was nobody there, of course.

Dan Pringle started for the mill, intending to denounce Aceria up one side and down the other. But he cooled off on the way. He began to grin and arrived feeling like a triumphal procession.

He looked around to see that nobody was within hearing, and called softly: "Aceria!"

There she was, between two piles. Pringle accused: "I suppose it was you who appeared to my wife just now?"

"I am afraid yes. I do not like to interfere in the affairs of mortals. But I had to teach you not to try to move my boards."

Pringle grinned. "That's okay, little lady. Don't give it a thought. You did me a favor. If I can count on my wife staying away awhile, maybe I can really enjoy life. So better not try any more stunts, or they're liable to backfire."

"You are still determined to break up my home?"

"Yep. Might have gotten soft-hearted if you hadn't pulled all these stunts. But now that lumber's going out if it's the last thing I do."

"I warn you, Mr. Pringle. I have some more stunts, as you call them."

"Such as?"

"You will see."

Pringle's pride—at least, the quality that his competitors called his orneriness—prevented him from giving in.

He could not let things go on as they were; the turmoil at the mill was costing him money every day, and he operated on a slim margin of profit. So next day he called all his mill workers together. They assembled in a silence made obtrusive by the lack of the band saw's shriek. Pringle called for volunteers for a risky job.

Those who had not experienced the athletic boards had heard about them and were not too anxious to learn more firsthand. But Pringle offered time and a half, and they had to eat. Twenty-one responded. Pringle had decided against the use of rollers. Most of the gang would simply sit on Pile No. 1040 to hold the boards down, and four men would carry each board across the intervening piles to the box car.

The boards tugged and wiggled a bit first, but Larochelle hit them with his ax and they went along. All went well until the car had been partly filled. Then there was an outbreak of yells from the car. Seconds later Michod and a man named Chisholm popped out of it, scrambled up the nearest pile to the tramway, and raced along the trestle. After them flew a short length of board. It swung this way and that, exactly as if somebody were chasing the two men and trying to hit them with it.

Pringle knew very well who was on the rear end of that piece of board, but he could not think of anything to do. While he watched, the board dropped lifeless to the tramway. Then there was a mighty clatter from the car, and most of the load of one-inch FAS maple spilled out the open car door on the side away from the piles. The boards, instead of being nice and rigid, like respectable maple planks, were writhing like a nestful of loathsome larvae. As they flopped out onto the cinders, they bent into semicircles like bows, then straightened out with a snap and soared off toward the woods.

"After 'em!" yelled Pringle. "You, Joe! Two bits a board for every one that's brought back!"

He scrambled down and set out after his lumber as fast as his short legs would carry him. Larochelle followed. The crew's nerves, already shaken by the sight of the unnatural pursuit of Michod and Chisholm, were now completely demoralized. But a few men followed Pringle and Larochelle.

They ran and they ran, tripping over logs and falling into brooks. Eventually Aceria ran out of ectoplasm, or something, and the boards ceased their bounding flight. They were gathered up in armfuls and brought back. They were piled on No. 1040 again. The men flatly refused to enter the box car with them, where there would be no room to dodge. It took all Pringle's authority and gifts of leadership to get them to go back to work at all; the scream of the saw did not ring out over hill and pond again until after the noon hour.

After lunch, Pringle hopped about the mill yard nervously, awaiting the counterattack, which he was sure was coming. It came soon enough. A mill like Pringle's, which is not equipped for turning out little things like chessmen, accumulates a vast amount of waste. Some of the slabs and edgings can be used as boiler fuel; some can be sold locally as firewood. But there is a surplus, and also a lot of useless sawdust. On the edge of the mill yard stood a pile of sawdust twenty feet high, waiting to be fed into the waste burner, a huge sheet-iron incinerator.

Presently this pile of sawdust did a curious thing. It swirled up into a whirling, top-shaped cloud, as if a whirlwind had settled on its apex. The cloud grew until there was no more sawdust on the ground, and the cloud was as big as a house. Then it swooped hither and thither about the yard. It hid the workers from each other and stung their faces. They were not encouraged when one of them pointed out that, while the cloud itself seemed to be borne on a miniature tornado, the far-off trees stood stiff in still air. They stampeded, yelling, into the sawmill. The engineer, hearing the tumult, prudently shut down the engine, and again the band saw and the edging, trimming, and slashing saws fell silent. Nobody else was silent. Pringle, rubbing sawdust out of his bloodshot eyes, could not make himself heard at all.

The cloud made a couple of tentative rushes at the mill. But Aceria's powers were apparently not equal to getting it in a lot of separate doors and windows and re-forming it inside. It hovered, teetering and swooshing menacingly, about the yard.

Many people did not love Dan Pringle, but they admitted that he had what it takes. He got the sneezing and blaspheming Larochelle and Fassler aside and sent them on an errand. They went out and ran to Fassler's car. The cloud swooped after them, but they jumped in and cranked up the windows, and off they went.

When they came back, they had two boxes full of colored sunglasses with little metal shields that made passable goggles out of them. Fassler said: "That's all there are of these things around here. We went clear up to Old Forge and cleaned out the stores. And my car stopped just before we got back. Sawdust in the carburetor."

Pringle yelled for attention. He put on a pair of the goggles, tied a handkerchief over the lower part of his face, turned up his shirt collar, pulled his hat down over his ears, and said:

"Now, if you guys have got any guts, you'll do like me and go out there and get back to work. The sawdust can't hurt you. I'm going out if I have to load the damn cars myself. Who's with me? Time and a half as long as that cloud's around."

Nobody said anything for a minute. Then Edward Gallivan mumbled something and put on a pair of goggles. Most of the others did likewise. They were, after all, a strong, tough lot, and the sight of their fat and aging boss preparing to face the cloud alone may have shamed them.

So, masked and goggled, they went back down the tramways, clutching at the piles for support as the whirlwind buffeted them and the sawdust stung every exposed inch of skin. Pringle grinned behind his handkerchief as he watched them get slowly on with their work, while Aceria's top shrieked about their ears. So, the wood spook still thought she could lick him? If this was her last stunt, he'd won, by jeepers. Or at least it was still a draw.

But it was not Aceria's last stunt. The cloud rose up and up until it looked no bigger than a marble. Everybody thought it was leaving for good, although they continued to glance up nervously at it.

Then it started down again. As it came near, they saw that it was a lot smaller and more opaque than when it had gone up. As it approached, it resolved itself into something that might be imagined by a paleontologist with the D. T.'s It looked somewhat like a pterodactyl, somewhat like an octopus, and somewhat like Fafner in "Siegfried." It had huge batlike wings and six long tentacular limbs with hands on their ends.

The shouts that had sounded on previous occasions about the yard were but as the chirp of canaries compared with the yells that now arose. As the thing glided over the yard, workers, foreman, inspectors, everybody went away. They went in straight radial lines, like droplets of mercury when a gob falls on a table top, only much faster. They jumped fences and waded neck-deep across the Moose River. Those inside the mill looked out to see what was up. They saw, and they went, too.

Pringle danced on the tramway. "Come back!" he screamed. "It can't hurt you. It's only sawdust! Look!" The monster was bobbing up and down in front of him, moving its horrid yellow jaws. He strode up to it and punched it. His fist went right through the sawdust, which swirled out in little puffs around his wrist. The hole made by his fist closed up as soon as he drew his arm back. For it was, as he surmised, merely the same cloud of animated sawdust, somewhat condensed and molded into this horrifying form.

"Look here! It's not a real thing at all! Come on back!" He passed his hand right through one of its groping limbs, which joined together again immediately.

But there was nobody to appreciate this display of nerve. Across the river, Pringle could see the rear elevation of a couple of small figures in drab work clothes, getting smaller every minute. As he watched, they disappeared into the forest. The form floated low over the site of the sawdust pile and collapsed. The pile was back where it had been, and Pringle was alone.

The thing that perhaps annoyed Pringle the most was that this time the engineer had run off without shutting down the engines, so that all the saws were whirling merrily in the empty mill. Pringle had to go down and turn the valve himself.

It was almost dark when Pringle and Larochelle appeared at the sawmill. They looked odd. Pringle was wearing, among other things, a catcher's mask and chest protector. Larochelle wore an old football helmet, several sweaters, and a lumber-yard worker's heavy leather apron. Pringle carried a flashlight; Larochelle, a five-gallon can of kerosene and a gasoline blowtorch.

"What are you going to do, Mr. Pringle?" asked Aceria. She was sitting on No. 1040. Larochelle had gone off to start the water pump and uncoil the fire hose.

"Going to have a little fire."

"You are going to burn my home?"

"Maybe."

"Won't you burn up the whole yard?"

"Not if we can help it. We're going to wet down the neighboring piles first. It's taking a chance, but what the hell?"

"Why are you so determined to destroy my home?"

"Because, damn it," Pringle's voice rose, "I've had all I can stand of this business! It's cost me a hundred times the value of those boards. But I won't give in to you, see? You won't let me load the boards. Okay, they're no good to me. So I might as well burn 'em up and end this nonsense for good. And you can't stop me. Your boards are tied down so you can't crawl inside 'em and animate 'em. Joe and I are protected, so it won't do you any good to get rough with us. And your sawdust monsters won't have a chance against this blowtorch."

Aceria was silent for a while. The only sounds were the hum of insects, the slap of Pringle's hand as he hit a punkie on his cheek, the whir of an automobile on the state highway, and Joe Larochelle's distant footsteps.

Then she said: "I do not think you will burn my home, Mr. Pringle."

"Who's going to stop me?"

"I am. You were very clever and very brave about facing my magics, no? And now you say, 'Ho-ho, I have beaten all Aceria's tricks.'"

"Yep." Pringle had been making a heap of edgings and bark, well away from the pile. A loud swish in the dark showed that Joe had begun his wetting down. "Now, Joe," Pringle called, "you catch the other end of this rope. We want to tighten up on the pile as soon as we pull a couple of boards out, so the rest can't get loose."

"Okay, Mr. Pringle. Here goes." There were sounds in the semidark as the two men moved around the pile, making sure that their enterprise would suffer neither from spreading of the flames nor unwonted activity on the part of the boards.

"Very clever," continued Aceria, "but I should have remembered sooner that it is not always the most complicated magic that is most effective."

"Uh," said Pringle. He splashed kerosene over his pile of kindling and lighted it. It flared up at once into a big, cheerful flame. "No wind," said Pringle, "so I guess she's safe enough. All right, Joe, let's haul the first board out."

Aceria seemed not to mind being ignored so pointedly. As Pringle and Larochelle laid hands on the board, she said:

"You were only so-so afraid of the boards when I went into them and made them alive, no? And you stood up to my monster. But there is something you are more afraid of than the boards or the monsters."

Pringle just grinned. "Is there? All right, Joe, heave! Don't pay any attention if I seem to be talking to myself."

"Yes. Union organizers," said Aceria.

"Huh?" Pringle stopped pulling on the board.

"Yes. You would like it, no, if *I* organized your men." Pringle's mouth dropped open.

"I could do it. I have been listening to them talk, and I know something about unions. And you know me. I appear, I disappear. You could not keep me away, like you do those men from the A. F. L. and the C. I. O. Oh, I would have a nice revenge for the burning of my home."

For the space of thirty seconds there was no sound but the breathing of the two men and the crackle of the flames. When Pringle made a noise, it was a ghastly strangling sound, like the death rattle of a man dying of thirst in the desert.

"You—" he said. And again, "You—"

"You sick, Mr. Pringle?" asked Larochelle.

"No," said Pringle, "I'm dying."

"Well?" spoke Aceria.

Pringle sat down heavily in the muck, took off his wire mask, and buried his face in his hands. "Go away, Joe," he said, and would listen to no remonstrances from the alarmed Larochelle.

Pringle said: "You win. What do you want me to do with the damn boards? We can't just leave 'em sit here until they rot."

"I would like them put in some nice dry place. I do not mind having them sold, if they are kept together until I can find another tree of the right kind."

"Let's see," said Pringle. "Earl Delacroix needs a new dance floor in his joint. But Earl's so tight he'll wait till somebody falls through the old one. Maybe if I offered him the boards at half price—or even a quarter—"

So it came to pass that, three weeks later, Earl Delacroix surprised those who knew his penurious habits by installing a new dance floor in The Pines. He surprised them somewhat less by hiring a luscious, red-haired girl as hostess. He himself was not too pleased over that innovation. But Pringle had brought the girl in personally and given her the strongest recommendation. Delacroix's mental eyebrows had gone up a bit. Hadn't Pringle's wife left him a while before? Oh, well, it was none of his business. If Pringle, who owned most of the town, wanted a —friend—employed, it was a good idea to employ the friend, without asking too many questions.

Delacroix had been particularly intrigued when the girl gave her name as Aceria; then, when he asked her full name, a whispered consultation between the girl and Pringle produced the surname of Jones. Jones, eh? Heh, heh.

Since then, Aceria has worked at The Pines. For appearance's sake, she has a room in the boarding house next door. But its bed is never slept in. Her landlady does not know that, every night, Aceria returns to the restaurant. It is dark then, and nobody is there to see her do whatever she does to merge herself with the floor boards. Probably she just fades out of sight. On these nocturnal trips, she always wears her old green dress. Or rather, it was green, but with the coming of fall it gradually turned a rich orange-yellow.

She dances divinely, and the local boys like her but find her a little odd. For instance, sooner or later she asks every acquaintance whether he knows of a place where a Norway maple grows. She is still asking, and if you know of one I am sure she would be grateful if you would inform her . . .

NOTHING
IN THE RULES

Not many spectators turn out for a meet between two minor women's swimming clubs, and this one was no exception. Louis Connaught, looking up at the balcony, thought casually that the single row of seats around it was about half full, mostly with the usual bored-looking assortment of husbands and boy friends, and some of the Hotel Creston's guests who had wandered in for want of anything better to do. One of the bellboys was asking an evening-gowned female not to smoke, and she was showing irritation. Mr. Santalucia and the little Santalucias were there as usual to see mamma perform. They waved down at Connaught.

Connaught—a dark devilish-looking little man—glanced over to the other side of the pool. The girls were coming out of the shower rooms, and their shrill conversation was blurred by the acoustics of the pool room into a continuous buzz. The air was faintly steamy. The stout party in white duck pants was Laird, coach of the Knickerbockers and Connaught's arch rival. He saw Connaught and boomed: "Hi, Louie!" The words rattled from wall to wall with a sound like a stick being drawn swiftly along a picket fence. Wambach of the A. A. U. Committee, who was refereeing, came in with his overcoat still on and greeted Laird, but the booming reverberations drowned his words before they got over to Connaught.

Then somebody else came through the door; or rather, a knot of people crowded through it all at once, facing inward, some in bathing suits and some in street clothes. It was a few seconds before Coach Connaught saw what they were looking at. He blinked and looked more closely, standing with his mouth half open.

But not for long. *"Hey!"* he yelled in a voice that made the pool room sound like the inside of a snare drum in use. "Protest! PROTEST! *You can't do that!"*

It had been the preceding evening when Herbert Laird opened his front door and shouted, "H'lo, Mark, come on in." The chill March wind was making a good deal of racket but not so much as all that. Laird was given to shouting on general principles. He was stocky and bald.

Mark Vining came in and deposited his brief case. He was younger than Laird—just thirty, in fact—with octagonal glasses and rather thin severe features, which made him look more serious than he was.

"Glad you could come, Mark," said Laird. "Listen, can you make our meet with the Crestons tomorrow night?"

Vining pursed his lips thoughtfully. "I guess so. Loomis decided not to appeal, so I don't have to work nights for a few days anyhow. Is something special up?"

Laird looked sly. "Maybe. Listen, you know that Mrs. Santalucia that Louie Connaught has been cleaning up with for the past couple of years? I think I've got that fixed. But I want you along to think up legal reasons why my scheme's okay."

"Why," said Vining cautiously, "what's your scheme?"

"Can't tell you now. I promised not to. But if Louie

can win by entering a freak—a woman with webbed fingers—"

"Oh, look here, Herb, you know those webs don't really help her—"

"Yes, yes, I know all the arguments. You've already got more water resistance to your arms than you've got muscle to overcome it with, and so forth. But I know Mrs. Santalucia has webbed fingers, and I know she's the best damned woman swimmer in New York. And I don't like it. It's bad for my prestige as a coach." He turned and shouted into the gloom: "Iantha!"

"Yes?"

"Come here, will you please? I want you to meet my friend Mr. Vining. Here, we need some light."

The light showed the living room as usual buried under disorderly piles of boxes of bathing suits and other swimming equipment, the sale of which furnished Herbert Laird with most of his income. It also showed a young woman coming in in a wheel chair.

One look gave Vining a feeling that, he knew, boded no good for him. He was unfortunate in being a pushover for any reasonably attractive girl and at the same time being cursed with an almost pathological shyness where women were concerned. The fact that both he and Laird were bachelors and took their swimming seriously were the main ties between them.

This girl was more than reasonably attractive. She was, thought the dazzled Vining, a wow, a ten-strike, a direct sixteen-inch hit. Her smooth, rather flat features and high cheekbones had a hint of Asian or American Indian and went oddly with her light-gold hair, which, Vining could have sworn, had a faint greenish tinge. A blanket was wrapped around her legs.

He came out of his trance as Laird introduced the exquisite creature as "Miss Delfoiros."

Miss Delfoiros did not seem exactly overcome. As she

extended her hand, she said with a noticeable accent: "You are not from the newspapers, Mr. Vining?"

"No," said Vining. "Just a lawyer. I specialize in wills and probates and things. Not thinking of drawing up yours, are you?"

She relaxed visibly and laughed. "No. I 'ope I shall not need one for a long, long time."

"Still," said Vining seriously, "you never know—"

Laird bellowed: "Wonder what's keeping that sister of mine. Dinner ought to be ready. *Martha!*" He marched out, and Vining heard Miss Laird's voice, something about "—but Herb, I had to let those things cool down—"

Vining wondered with a great wonder what he should say to Miss Delfoiros. Finally he said, "Smoke?"

"Oh, no, thank you very much. I do not do it."

"Mind if I do?"

"No, not at all."

"Whereabouts do you hail from?" Vining thought the question sounded both brusque and silly. He never did get the hang of talking easily under these circumstances.

"Oh, I am from Kip—Cyprus, I mean. You know, the island."

"Will you be at this swimming meet?"

"Yes, I think so."

"You don't"—he lowered his voice—"know what scheme Herb's got up his sleeve to beat La Santalucia?"

"Yes . . . no . . . I do not . . . what I mean is, I must not tell."

More mystery, thought Vining. What he really wanted to know was why she was confined to a wheel chair; whether the cause was temporary or permanent. But you couldn't ask a person right out, and he was still trying to concoct a leading question when Laird's bellow wafted in: "All right, folks, soup's on!" Vining would have pushed the wheel chair in, but before he had a chance, the girl had spun the chair around and was halfway to the dining room.

Vining said: "Hello, Martha, how's the schoolteaching business?" But he was not really paying much attention to Laird's capable spinster sister. He was gauping at Miss Delfoiros, who was quite calmly emptying a teaspoonful of salt into her water glass and stirring.

"What . . . what?" he gulped.

"I 'ave to," she said. "Fresh water makes me—like what you call drunk."

"Listen, Mark!" roared his friend. "Are you sure you can be there on time tomorrow night? There are some questions of eligibility to be cleared up, and I'm likely to need you badly."

"Will Miss Delfoiros be there?" Vining grinned, feeling very foolish inside.

"Oh, sure. Iantha's our . . . say, listen, you know that little eighteen-year-old Clara Havranek? She did the hundred in one-oh-five yesterday. She's championship material. We'll clean the Creston Club yet—" He went on, loud and fast, about what he was going to do to Louie Connaught's girls. The while, Mark Vining tried to concentrate on his own food, which was good, and on Iantha Delfoiros, who was charming but evasive.

There seemed to be something special about Miss Delfoiros' food, to judge by the way Martha Laird had served it. Vining looked closely and saw that it had the peculiarly dead and clammy look that a dinner once hot but now cold has. He asked about it.

"Yes," she said, "I like it cold."

"You mean you don't eat *anything* hot?"

She made a face. " 'Ot food? No, I do not like it. To us it is—"

"Listen, Mark! I hear the W. S. A. is going to throw a post-season meet in April for novices only—"

Vining's dessert lay before him a full minute before

he noticed it. He was too busy thinking how delightful Miss Delfoiros' accent was.

When dinner was over, Laird said, "Listen, Mark, you know something about these laws against owning gold? Well, look here—" He led the way to a candy box on a table in the living room. The box contained, not candy, but gold and silver coins. Laird handed the lawyer several of them. The first one he examined was a silver crown, bearing the inscription "Carolus II Dei Gra" encircling the head of England's Merry Monarch with a wreath in his hair—or, more probably, in his wig. The second was an eighteenth-century Spanish dollar. The third was a Louis d'Or.

"I didn't know you went in for coin collecting, Herb," said Vining. "I suppose these are all genuine?"

"They're genuine all right. But I'm not collecting 'em. You might say I'm taking 'em in trade. I have a chance to sell ten thousand bathing caps, if I can take payment in those things."

"I shouldn't think the U. S. Rubber Company would like the idea much."

"That's just the point. What'll I do with 'em after I get 'em? Will the government put me in jail for having 'em?"

"You needn't worry about that. I don't think the law covers old coins, though I'll look it up to make sure. Better call up the American Numismatic Society—they're in the 'phone book—and they can tell you how to dispose of them. But look here, what the devil is this? Ten thousand bathing caps to be paid for in pieces-of-eight? I never heard of such a thing."

"That's it exactly. Just ask the little lady here." Laird turned to Iantha, who was nervously trying to signal him to keep quiet. "The deal's her doing."

"I did . . . did—" She looked as if she were going to

cry. " 'Erbert, you should not have said that. You see," she said to Vining, "we do not like to 'ave a lot to do with people. Always it causes us troubles."

"Who," asked Vining, "do you mean by 'we'?"

She shut her mouth obstinately. Vining almost melted, but his legal instincts came to the surface. If you don't get a grip on yourself, he thought, you'll be in love with her in another five minutes, and that might be a disaster. He said firmly:

"Herb, the more I see of this business, the crazier it looks. Whatever's going on, you seem to be trying to get me into it. But I'm damned if I'll let you unless I know what it's all about."

"Might as well tell him, Iantha," said Laird. "He'll know when he sees you swim tomorrow, anyhow."

She said: "You will not tell the newspaper men, Mr. Vining?"

"No, I won't say anything to anybody."

"You promise?"

"Of course. You can depend on a lawyer to keep things under his hat."

"Under his—I suppose you mean not to tell. So, look." She reached down and pulled up the lower end of the blanket.

Vining looked. Where he expected to see feet, there was a pair of horizontal flukes, like those of a porpoise.

Louis Connaught's having kittens, when he saw what his rival coach had sprung on him, can thus be easily explained. First he doubted his own senses; then he doubted whether there was any justice in the world.

Meanwhile, Mark Vining proudly pushed Iantha's wheel chair in among the cluster of judges and time-keepers at the starting end of the pool. Iantha herself, in a bright green bathing cap, held her blanket around her shoulders, but the slate-gray tail with its flukes was plain for all to see. The skin of the tail was smooth and the flukes were horizontal; artists who show mermaids with scales and a vertical tail fin, like a fish's, simply do not know their zoölogy.

"All right, all right," bellowed Laird. "Don't crowd around. Everybody get back to where they belong. Everybody, please."

One of the spectators, leaning over the rail of the balcony to see, dropped a fountain pen into the pool. One of Connaught's girls, a Miss Black, dove in after it.

Ogden Wambach, the referee, poked a finger at the skin of the tail. He was a well-groomed, gray-haired man.

"Laird," he said, "is this a joke?"

"Not at all. She's entered in the back stroke and all the free styles, just like any other club member. She's even registered with the A. A. U."

"But . . . but . . . I mean, is it alive? Is it real?"

Iantha spoke up. "Why do you not ask me those questions, Mr. . . . Mr. . . . I do not know you—"

"Good grief," said Wambach. "It talks! I'm the referee, Miss—"

"Delfoiros. Iantha Delfoiros."

"My word. Upon my word. That means—let's see— Violet Porpoise-tail, doesn't it? *Delphis* plus *oura*—"

"You know Greek? Oh, 'ow nice!" She broke into a string of *dimotiki*.

Wambach gulped a little. "Too fast for me, I'm afraid. And that's *modern* Greek, isn't it?"

"Why, yes. I am modern, am I not?"

"Dear me. I suppose so. But is that tail really real? I mean, it's not just a piece of costumery?"

"Oh, but yes." Iantha threw off the blanket and waved her flukes. Everyone in the pool seemed to have turned into a pair of eyeballs to which a body and a pair of legs was vaguely attached.

"Dear me," said Ogden Wambach. "Where are my

glasses? You understand, I just want to make sure there's nothing spurious about this."

Mrs. Santalucia, a muscular-looking lady with a visible mustache and fingers webbed down to the first joint, said, "You mean I gotta swim against *her?*"

Louis Connaught had been sizzling like a dynamite fuse. "You can't do it!" he shrilled. "This is a woman's meet! I protest!"

"So what?" said Laird.

"But you can't enter a fish in a woman's swimming meet! Can you, Mr. Wambach?"

Mark Vining spoke up. He had just taken a bunch of papers clipped together out of his pocket, and was running through them.

"Miss Delfoiros," he asserted, "is not a fish. She's a mammal."

"How do you figure that?" yelled Connaught.

"*Look* at her."

"Um-m-m," said Ogden Wambach. "I see what you mean."

"But," howled Connaught, "she still ain't human!"

"There is a question about that, Mr. Vining," said Wambach.

"No question at all. There's nothing in the rules against entering a mermaid, and there's nothing that says the competitors have to be human."

Connaught was hopping about like an overwrought cricket. He was now waving a copy of the current A. A. U. swimming, diving, and water polo rules. "I still protest! Look here! All through here it only talks about two kinds of meets, men's and women's. She ain't a woman, and she certainly ain't a man. If the Union had wanted to have meets for mermaids they'd have said so."

"Not a woman?" asked Vining in a manner that juries learned meant a rapier thrust at an opponent. "I beg your pardon, Mr. Connaught. I looked the question up."

He frowned at his sheaf of papers. "Webster's International Dictionary, Second Edition, defines a woman as 'any female person.' And it further defines 'person' as 'a being characterized by conscious apprehension, rationality, and a moral sense.'" He turned to Wambach. "Sir, I think you'll agree that Miss Delfoiros has exhibited conscious apprehension and rationality during her conversation with you, won't you?"

"My word . . . I really don't know what to say, Mr. Vining . . . I suppose she has, but I couldn't say—"

Horwitz, the scorekeeper, spoke up. "You might ask her to give the multiplication table." Nobody paid him any attention.

Connaught exhibited symptoms of apoplexy. "But you can't— What the hell you talking about—conscious apap—"

"Please, Mr. Connaught!" said Wambach. "When you shout that way I can't understand you because of the echoes."

Connaught mastered himself with a visible effort. Then he looked crafty. "How do I know she's got a moral sense?"

Vining turned to Iantha. "Have you ever been in jail, Iantha?"

Iantha laughed. "What a funny question, Mark! But of course, I have not."

"That's what *she* says," sneered Connaught. "How you gonna prove it?"

"We don't have to," said Vining loftily. "The burden of proof is on the accuser, and the accused is legally innocent until proved guilty. That principle was well established by the time of King Edward the First."

"Oh, damn King Edward the First," cried Connaught. "That wasn't the kind of moral sense I meant anyway. How about what they call moral turp-turp— You know what I mean."

"Hey," growled Laird, "what's the idea? Are you trying to cast— What's the word, Mark?"

"Aspersions?"

"—cast aspersions on one of my swimmers? You watch out, Louie. If I hear you be— What's the word, Mark?"

"Besmirching her fair name?"

"—besmirching her fair name, I'll drown you in your own tank."

"And after that," said Vining, "we'll slap a suit on you for slander."

"Gentlemen! Gentlemen!" said Wambach. "Let's not have any more personalities, please. This is a swimming meet, not a lawsuit. Let's get to the point."

"We've made ours," said Vining with dignity. "We've shown that Iantha Delfoiros is a woman, and Mr. Connaught has stated, himself, that this is a woman's meet. Therefore, Miss Delfoiros is eligible. Q. E. D."

"Ahem," said Wambach. "I don't quite know—I never had a case like this to decide before."

Louis Connaught almost had tears in his eyes; at least he sounded as if he did. "Mr. Wambach, you can't let Herb Laird do this to me. I'll be a laughingstock."

Laird snorted. "How about your beating me with your Mrs. Santalucia? I didn't get any sympathy from you when people laughed at me on account of that. And how much good did it do me to protest against her fingers?"

"But," wailed Connaught, "if he can enter this Miss Delfoiros, what's to stop somebody from entering a trained sea lion or something? Do you want to make competitive swimming into a circus?"

Laird grinned. "Go ahead, Louie. Nobody's stopping you from entering anything you like. How about it, Ogden? Is she a woman?"

"Well . . . really . . . oh, dear—"

"Please!" Iantha Delfoiros rolled her violet-blue eyes

at the bewildered referee. "I should so like to swim in this nice pool with all these nice people!"

Wambach sighed. "All right, my dear, you shall!"

"Whoopee!" cried Laird, the cry being taken up by Vining, the members of the Knickerbocker Swimming Club, the other officials, and lastly the spectators. The noise in the inclosed space made sensitive eardrums wince.

"Wait a minute," yelped Connaught when the echoes had died. "Look here, page 19 of the rules. 'Regulation Costume, Women: Suits must be of dark color, with skirt attached. Leg is to reach—' and so forth. Right here it says it. She can't swim the way she is, not in a sanctioned meet."

"That's true," said Wambach. "Let's see—"

Horwitz looked up from his little score-sheet littered table. "Maybe one of the girls has a halter she could borrow," he suggested. "That would be something."

"Halter, phooey!" snapped Connaught. "This means a regular suit with legs and a skirt, and everybody knows it."

"But she hasn't got any legs!" cried Laird. "How could she get into—"

"That's just the point! If she can't wear a suit with legs, and the rules say you gotta have legs, she can't wear the regulation suit, and she can't compete! I gotcha that time! Ha-ha, I'm sneering!"

"I'm afraid not, Louie," said Vining, thumbing his own copy of the rule-book. He held it up to the light and read: " 'Note.—These rules are approximate, the idea being to bar costumes which are immodest, or will attract undue attention and comment. The referee shall have the power'—et cetera, et cetera. If we cut the legs out of a regular suit, and she pulled the rest of it on over her head, that would be modest enough for all practical purposes. Wouldn't it, Mr. Wambach?"

"Dear me—I don't know—I suppose it would."

Laird hissed to one of his pupils, "Hey, listen, Miss Havranek! You know where my suitcase is? Well, you get one of the extra suits out of it, and there's a pair of scissors in with the first-aid things. You fix that suit up so Iantha can wear it."

Connaught subsided. "I see now," he said bitterly, "why you guys wanted to finish with a 300-yard free style instead of a relay. If I'd 'a' known what you were planning—and, you, Mark Vining, if I ever get in a jam, I'll go to jail before I hire you for a lawyer, so help me!"

Mrs. Santalucia had been glowering at Iantha Delfoiros. Suddenly she turned to Connaught. "Thissa no fair. I swim against people. I no-gotta swim against mermaids."

"Please, Maria, don't *you* desert me," wailed Connaught.

"I no swim tonight."

Connaught looked up appealingly to the balcony. Mr. Santalucia and the little Santalucias, guessing what was happening, burst into a chorus of: "Go on, mamma! You show them, mamma!"

"Aw right. I swim one, maybe two races. If I see I no got a chance, I no swim no more."

"That's better, Maria. It wouldn't really count if she beat you anyway." Connaught headed for the door, saying something about "telephone" on the way.

Despite the delays in starting the meet, nobody left the pool room through boredom. In fact, the empty seats in the balcony were full by this time and people were standing up behind them. Word had gotten around the Hotel Creston that something was up.

By the time Louis Connaught returned, Laird and Vining were pulling the altered bathing suit on over Iantha's head. It did not reach quite so far as they expected, having been designed for a slightly slimmer swimmer. Not that Iantha was fat. But her human part, if not exactly plump, was at least comfortably upholstered, so that no bones showed. Iantha squirmed around in the suit a good deal and threw a laughing remark in Greek to Wambach, whose expression showed that he hoped it did not mean what he suspected it did.

Laird said, "Now listen, Iantha, remember not to move till the gun goes off. And remember that you swim directly over the black line on the bottom, not between two lines."

"Are they going to shoot a gun? Oh, I am afraid of shooting!"

"It's nothing to be afraid of; just blank cartridges. They don't hurt anybody. And it won't be so loud inside that cap."

"Herb," said Vining, "won't she lose time getting off, not being able to make a flat dive like the others?"

"She will. But it won't matter. She can swim a mile in *four* minutes, without really trying."

Ritchey, the starter, announced the fifty-yard free style. He called: "All right, everybody, line up."

Iantha slithered off her chair and crawled over to the starting platform. The other girls were all standing with feet together, bodies bent forward at the hips and arms pointing backward. Iantha got into a curious position of her own, with her tail bent under her and her weight resting on her hand and flukes.

"Hey! Protest!" shouted Connaught. "The rules say that all races, except back strokes, are started with dives. What kind of a dive do you call that?"

"Oh, dear," said Wambach. "What—"

"That," said Vining urbanely, "is a mermaid dive. You couldn't expect her to stand upright on her tail."

"But that's just it!" cried Connaught. "First you enter a non-regulation swimmer. Then you put a non-regulation suit on her. Then you start her off with a non-regulation dive. Ain't there anything you guys do like other people?"

"But," said Vining, looking through the rule book, "it doesn't say—here it is. 'The start in all races shall be made with a dive.' But there's nothing in the rules about what kind of dive shall be used. And the dictionary defines a dive simply as 'a plunge into water.' So if you jump in feet first holding your nose, that's a dive for the purpose of the discussion. And in my years of watching swimming meets, I've seen some funnier starting dives than Miss Delfoiros'."

"I suppose he's right," said Wambach.

"Okay, okay," snarled Connaught. "But the next time I have a meet with you and Herb, I bring a lawyer along too, see?"

Ritchey's gun went off. Vining noticed that Iantha flinched a little at the report and was perhaps slowed down a trifle in getting off by it. The other girls' bodies shot out horizontally to smack the water loudly, but Iantha slipped in with the smooth, unhurried motion of a diving seal. Lacking the advantage of feet to push off with, she was several yards behind the other swimmers before she really got started. Mrs. Santalucia had taken her usual lead, foaming along with the slow strokes of her webbed hands.

Iantha did not bother to come to the surface except at the turn, where she had been specifically ordered to come up so that the judge of the turns would not raise arguments as to whether she had touched the end, and at the finish. She hardly used her arms at all, except for an occasional flip of her trailing hands to steer her. The swift up-and-down flutter of the powerful tail flukes sent her through the water like a torpedo, her wake appearing on the surface six or eight feet behind her. As she shot through the as yet unruffled waters at the far end of the pool on the first leg, Vining, who had gone around to the side to watch, noticed that she had the power of closing her nostrils tightly under water, like a seal or a hippopotamus.

Mrs. Santalucia finished the race in the very creditable time of 29.8 seconds. But Iantha Delfoiros arrived, not merely first, but in the time of 8.0 seconds. At the finish she did not reach up to touch the starting platform and then hoist herself out by her arms the way human swimmers do. She simply angled up sharply, left the water like a leaping trout, and came down with a moist smack on the concrete, almost bowling over a timekeeper. By the time the other contestants had completed the turn she was sitting on the platform with her tail curled under her. As the girls foamed laboriously down the final leg, she smiled dazzlingly at Vining, who had had to run to be in at the finish.

"That," she said, "was much fun, Mark. I am so glad you and 'Erbert put me in these races."

Mrs. Santalucia climbed out and walked over to Horwitz's table. That young man was staring in disbelief at the figures he had just written.

"Yes," he said, "that's what it says. Miss Iantha Delfoiros, 8.0; Mrs. Maria Santalucia, 29.8. Please don't drip on my score sheets, lady. Say, Wambach, isn't this a world's record or something?"

"My word!" said Wambach. "It's less than half the existing short-course record. Less than a third, maybe; I'd have to check it. Dear me! I'll have to take it up with the Committee. I don't know whether they'd allow it; I don't think they will, even though there isn't any specific rule against mermaids."

Vining spoke up. "I think we've complied with all the requirements to have records recognized, Mr. Wambach. Miss Delfoiros was entered in advance like all the others."

"Yes, yes, Mr. Vining, but don't you see, a record's

a serious matter? No ordinary human being could ever come near a time like that."

"Unless he used an outboard motor," said Connaught. "If you allow contestants to use tail fins like Miss Delfoiros, you oughta let 'em use propellers. I don't see why these guys should be the only ones to be let bust rules all over the place, and then think up lawyer arguments why it's okay. I'm gonna get me a lawyer, too."

"That's all right, Ogden," said Laird. "You take it up with the Committee, but we don't really care much about the records anyway, so long as we can lick Louie here." He smiled indulgently at Connaught, who sputtered with fury.

"I no swim," announced Mrs. Santalucia. "This is all crazy business. I no got a chance."

"Now, Maria," said Connaught, taking her aside, "just once more, won't you please? My reputation—" The rest of his words were drowned in the general reverberation of the pool room. But at the end of them the redoubtable female appeared to have given in to his entreaties.

The hundred-yard free style started in much the same manner as the fifty-yard. Iantha did not flinch at the gun this time and got off to a good start. She skimmed along just below the surface, raising a wake like a tuna clipper. These waves confused the swimmer in the adjacent lane, who happened to be Miss Breitenfeld of the Creston Club. As a result, on her first return leg, Iantha met Miss Breitenfeld swimming athwart her—Iantha's—lane, and rammed the unfortunate girl amidships. Miss Breitenfeld went down without even a gurgle, spewing bubbles.

Connaught shrieked: "Foul! Foul!" although in the general uproar it sounded like "Wow! Wow!" Several swimmers who were not racing dove in to the rescue, and the race came to a stop in general confusion and pandemonium. When Miss Breitenfeld was hauled out, it was found that she had merely had the wind knocked out of her and had swallowed considerable water.

Mark Vining, looking around for Iantha, found her holding on to the edge of the pool and shaking her head. Presently she crawled out, crying:

"Is she 'urt? Is she 'urt? Oh, I am so sorree! I did not think there would be anybody in my lane, so I did not look ahead."

"See?" yelled Connaught. "See, Wambach? See what happens? They ain't satisfied to walk away with the races with their fish-woman. No, they gotta try to cripple my swimmers by butting their slats in. Herb," he went on nastily, "why dontcha get a pet swordfish? Then when you rammed one of my poor girls she'd be out of competition for good!"

"Oh," said Iantha, "I did not mean—it was an accident!"

"Accident my foot!"

"But it was. Mr. Referee, I do not want to bump people. My 'ead 'urts, and my neck also. You think I try to break my neck on purpose?" Iantha's altered suit had crawled up under her armpits, but nobody noticed particularly.

"Sure it was an accident," bellowed Laird. "Anybody could see that. And listen, if anybody was fouled it was Miss Delfoiros."

"Certainly," chimed in Vining. "She was in her own lane, and the other girl wasn't."

"Oh dear me," said Wambach. "I suppose they're right again. This'll have to be re-swum anyway. Does Miss Breitenfeld want to compete?"

Miss Breitenfeld did not, but the others lined up again. This time the race went off without untoward incident.

Iantha again made a spectacular leaping finish, just as the other three swimmers were halfway down the second of their four legs.

When Mrs. Santalucia emerged this time, she said to Connaught: "I no swim no more. That is final."

"Oh, but Maria—" It got him nowhere. Finally he said, "Will you swim in the races that she don't enter?"

"Is there any?"

"I think so. Hey, Horwitz, Miss Delfoiros ain't entered in the breast stroke, is she?"

Horwitz looked. "No, she isn't," he said.

"That's something. Say, Herb, how come you didn't put your fish-woman in the breast stroke?"

Vining answered for Laird. "Look at your rules, Louie. 'The feet shall be drawn up simultaneously, the knees bent and open,' et cetera. The rules for back stroke and free style don't say anything about how the legs shall be used, but those for breast stroke do. So no legs, no breast stroke. We aren't giving you a chance to make any legitimate protests."

"Legitimate protests!" Connaught turned away, sputtering.

While the dives were being run off, Vining, watching, became aware of an ethereal melody. First he thought it was in his head. Then he was sure it was coming from one of the spectators. He finally located the source; it was Iantha Delfoiros, sitting in her wheel chair and singing softly. By leaning nearer he could make out the words:

> "*Die schoenste Jungfrau sitzet*
> *Dort ober wunderbar;*
> *Ihr goldnes Geschmeide blitzet;*
> *Sie kaemmt ihr goldenes Haar.*"

Vining went over quietly. "Iantha," he said "Pull your bathing suit down, and don't sing."

She complied, looking up at him with a giggle. "But that is a nice song! I learn it from a wrecked German sailor. It is about one of my people."

"I know, but it'll distract the judges. They have to watch the dives closely, and the place is too noisy as it is."

"Such a nice man you are, Mark, but so serious!" She giggled again.

Vining wondered at the subtle change in the mermaid's manner. Then a horrible thought struck him.

"Herb!" he whispered. "Didn't she say something last night about getting drunk on fresh water?"

Laird looked up. "Yes. She— My God, the water in the pool's fresh! I never thought of that. Is she showing signs?"

"I think she is."

"Listen, Mark, what'll we do?"

"I don't know. She's entered in two more events, isn't she? Back stroke and 300-yard free style?"

"Yes."

"Well, why not withdraw her from the back stroke, and give her a chance to sober up before the final event?"

"Can't. Even with all her firsts, we aren't going to win by any big margin. Louie has the edge on us in the dives, and Mrs. Santalucia'll win the breast stroke. In the events Iantha's in, if she takes first and Louie's girls take second and third, that means five points for us but four for him, so we have an advantage of only one point. And her world's record time don't give us any more points."

"Guess we'll have to keep her in and take a chance," said Vining glumly.

Iantha's demeanor was sober enough in lining up for the back stroke. Again she lost a fraction of a second in getting started by not having feet to push off with. But once she got started, the contest was even more one-sided than the free-style races had been. The human part of her body was practically out of water, skimming the surface like the front half of a speedboat. She made paddling motions with her arms, but that was merely for technical reasons; the power was all furnished by the flukes. She did not jump out on to the starting-platform this time; for a flash Vining's heart almost stopped as the emerald-green bathing cap seemed about to crash into the tiles at the end of the pool. But Iantha had judged the distance to a fraction of an inch, and braked to a stop with her flukes just before striking.

The breast stroke was won easily by Mrs. Santalucia, although her slow, plodding stroke was less spectacular than the butterfly of her competitors. The shrill cheers of the little Santalucias could be heard over the general hubbub. When the winner climbed out, she glowered at Iantha and said to Connaught:

"Louie, if you ever put me in a meet wit' mermaids again, I no swim for you again, never. Now I go home." With which she marched off to the shower room.

Ritchey was just about to announce the final event, the 300-yard free style, when Connaught plucked his sleeve. "Jack," he said, "wait a second. One of my swimmers is gonna be delayed a coupla minutes." He went out a door.

Laird said to Vining: "Wonder what Louie's grinning about. He's got something nasty, I bet. He was 'phoning earlier, you remember."

"We'll soon see— What's that?" A hoarse bark wafted in from somewhere and rebounded from the walls.

Connaught reappeared carrying two buckets. Behind him was a little round man in three sweaters. Behind the little round man gallumped a glossy California sea lion. At the sight of the gently rippling, jade-green pool, the animal barked joyously and skidded into the water, swam swiftly about, and popped out on the landing platform, barking. The bark had a peculiarly nerve-racking effect in the echoing pool room.

Ogden Wambach seized two handfuls of his sleek gray hair and tugged. "Connaught!" he shouted. "What is that?"

"Oh, that's just one of my swimmers, Mr. Wambach."

"Hey, listen!" rumbled Laird. "We're going to protest this time. Miss Delfoiros is at least a woman, even if she's a kind of peculiar one. But you can't call *that* a woman."

Connaught grinned like Satan looking over a new shipment of sinners. "Didn't you just say to go ahead and enter a sea lion if I wanted to?"

"I don't remember saying—"

"Yes, Herbert," said Wambach, looking haggard. "You did say it. There didn't used to be any trouble in deciding whether a swimmer was a woman or not. But now that you've brought in Miss Delfoiros, there doesn't seem to be any place we can draw a line."

"But look here, Ogden, there is such a thing as going too far—"

"That's just what I said about you!" shrilled Connaught.

Wambach took a deep breath. "Let's not shout, please. Herbert, technically you may have an argument. But after we allowed Miss Delfoiros to enter, I think it would be only sporting to let Louie have his seal. Especially after you told him to get one if he could."

Vining spoke up. "Oh, we're always glad to do the sporting thing. But I'm afraid the sea lion wasn't entered at the beginning of the meet as is required by the rules. We don't want to catch hell from the Committee—"

"Oh, yes, she was," said Connaught. "See!" He pointed to one of Horwitz's sheets. "Her name's Alice Black, and there it is."

"But," protested Vining, "I thought *that* was Alice Black." He pointed to a slim dark girl in a bathing suit who was sitting on a window ledge.

"It is," grinned Connaught. "It's just a coincidence that they both got the same name."

"You don't expect us to believe *that?*"

"I don't care whether you believe or not. It's so. Ain't the sea lion's name Alice Black?" He turned to the little fat man, who nodded.

"Let it pass," moaned Wambach. "We can't take time off to get this animal's birth certificate."

"Well, then," said Vining, "how about the regulation suit? Maybe you'd like to try to put a suit on your sea lion?"

"Don't have to. She's got one already. It grows on her. Yah, yah, yah, gotcha that time."

"I suppose," said Wambach, "that you *could* consider a natural sealskin pelt as equivalent to a bathing suit."

"Sure you could. That's the point. Anyway, the idea of suits is to be modest, and nobody gives a damn about a sea lion's modesty."

Vining made a final point. "You refer to the animal as 'her,' but how do we know it's a female? Even Mr. Wambach wouldn't let you enter a male sea lion in a women's meet."

Wambach spoke: "How do you tell on a sea lion?"

Connaught looked at the little fat man. "Well, maybe we had better not go into that here. How would it be if I put up a ten-dollar bond that Alice is a female, and you checked on her sex later?"

"That seems fair," said Wambach.

Vining and Laird looked at each other. "Shall we let 'em get away with that, Mark?" asked the latter.

Vining rocked on his heels for a few seconds. Then he said, "I think we might as well. Can I see you outside a minute, Herb? You people don't mind holding up the race a couple of minutes more, do you? We'll be right back."

Connaught started to protest about further delay but thought better of it. Laird presently reappeared, looking unwontedly cheerful.

" 'Erbert!" said Iantha.

"Yes?" he put his head down.

"I'm afraid—"

"You're afraid Alice might bite you in the water? Well, I wouldn't want that—"

"Oh, no, not afraid that way. Alice, poof! If she gets nasty I give her one with the tail. But I am afraid she can swim faster than me."

"Listen, Iantha, you just go ahead and swim the best you can. Twelve legs, remember. And don't be surprised, no matter what happens."

"What you two saying?" asked Connaught suspiciously.

"None of your business, Louie. Whatcha got in that pail? *Fish?* I see how you're going to work this. Wanta give up and concede the meet now?"

Connaught merely snorted.

The only competitors in the 300-yard free-style race were Iantha Delfoiros and the sea lion, allegedly named Alice. The normal members of both clubs declared that nothing would induce them to get into the pool with the animal. Not even the importance of collecting a third-place point would move them.

Iantha got into her usual starting position. Beside her, the little round man maneuvered Alice, holding her by an improvised leash made of a length of rope. At the far end, Connaught had placed himself and one of the buckets.

Ritchey fired his gun; the little man slipped the leash and said: "Go get 'em, Alice!" Connaught took a fish out of his bucket and waved it. But Alice, frightened by the shot, set up a furious barking and stayed where she was. Not till Iantha had almost reached the far end of the pool did Alice sight the fish at the other end. Then she slid off and shot down the water like a streak. Those who have seen sea lions merely loafing about a pool in a zoo or aquarium have no conception of how fast they can go when they try. Fast as the mermaid was, the sea lion was faster. She made two bucking jumps out of water before she arrived and oozed out onto the concrete. One gulp and the fish had vanished.

Alice spotted the bucket and tried to get her head into it. Connaught fended her off as best he could with his feet. At the starting end, the little round man had taken a fish out of the other bucket and was waving it, calling: "Here Alice!"

Alice did not get the idea until Iantha had finished her second leg. Then she made up for lost time.

The same trouble occurred at the starting end of the pool; Alice failed to see why she should swim twenty-five yards for a fish when there were plenty of them a few feet away. The result was that, at the halfway-mark, Iantha was two legs ahead. But then Alice caught on. She caught up with and passed Iantha in the middle of her eighth leg, droozling out of the water at each end long enough to gulp a fish and then speeding down to the other end. In the middle of the tenth leg, she was ten yards ahead of the mermaid.

At that point, Mark Vining appeared through the door, running. In each hand he held a bowl of goldfish by the edge. Behind him came Miss Havranek and Miss Tufts, also of the Knickerbockers, both similarly burdened. The guests of the Hotel Creston had been mildly curious when a dark, severe-looking young man and two girls in bathing suits had dashed into the lobby and made off with the six bowls. But they had been too well-bred to inquire directly about the rape of the goldfish.

Vining ran down the side of the pool to a point near the far end. There he extended his arms and inverted the bowls. Water and fish cascaded into the pool. Miss Havranek and Miss Tufts did likewise at other points along the edge of the pool.

Results were immediate. The bowls had been large, and each had contained about six or eight fair-sized goldfish. The forty-odd bright-colored fish, terrified by their rough handling, darted hither and thither about the pool, or at least went as fast as their inefficient build would permit them.

Alice, in the middle of her ninth leg, angled off sharply. Nobody saw her snatch the fish; one second it was there, and the next it was not. Alice doubled with a swirl of flippers and shot diagonally across the pool. Another fish vanished. Forgotten were her master and Louis Connaught and their buckets. This was much more fun. Meanwhile, Iantha finished her race, narrowly avoiding a collision with the sea lion on her last leg.

Connaught hurled the fish he was holding as far as he could. Alice snapped it up and went on hunting. Connaught ran toward the starting-platform, yelling: "Foul! Foul! Protest! Protest! Foul! Foul!"

He arrived to find the timekeepers comparing watches on Iantha's swim, Laird and Vining doing a kind of war dance, and Ogden Wambach looking like the March Hare on the twenty-eighth of February.

"Stop!" cried the referee. "Stop, Louie! If you shout like that you'll drive me mad! I'm almost mad now! I know what you're going to say."

"Well . . . well . . . why don't you do something, then? Why don't you tell these crooks where to head in? Why don't you have 'em expelled from the Union? Why don't you—"

"Relax, Louie," said Vining. "We haven't done anything illegal."

"*What?* Why, you dirty—"

"Easy, easy." Vining looked speculatively at his fist. The little man followed his glance and quieted somewhat. "There's nothing in the rules about putting fish into a pool. Intelligent swimmers, like Miss Delfoiros, know enough to ignore them when they're swimming a race."

"But—what—why you—"

Vining walked off, leaving the two coaches and the referee to fight it out. He looked for Iantha. She was sitting on the edge of the pool, paddling in the water with her flukes. Beside her were four feebly flopping goldfish laid out in a row on the tiles. As he approached, she picked one up and put the front end of it in her mouth. There was a flash of pearly teeth and a spasmodic flutter of the fish's tail, and the front half of the fish was gone. The other half followed immediately.

At that instant Alice spotted the three remaining fish. The sea lion had cleaned out the pool and was now slithering around on the concrete, barking and looking for more prey. She gallumped past Vining toward the mermaid.

Iantha saw her coming. The mermaid hoisted her tail out of the water, pivoted where she sat, swung the tail up in a curve, and brought the flukes down on the sea lion's head with a loud *spat*. Vining, who was twenty feet off, could have sworn he felt the wind of the blow.

Alice gave a squawk of pain and astonishment and slithered away, shaking her head. She darted past Vining again, and for reasons best known to herself hobbled over to the center of argument and bit Ogden Wambach in the leg. The referee screeched and climbed up on Horwitz's table.

"Hey," said the scorekeeper. "You're scattering my papers!"

"I still say they're publicity-hunting crooks!" yelled

Connaught, waving his copy of the rule book at Wambach.

"Bunk!" bellowed Laird. "He's just sore because we can think up more stunts than he can. He started it, with his web-fingered woman."

"Damn your complaints!" screamed Wambach. "Damn your sea lions! Damn your papers! Damn your mermaids! Damn your web-fingered women! Damn your swimming clubs! Damn all of you! I'm going mad! You hear? Mad, mad, mad! One more word out of either of you and I'll have you suspended from the Union!"

"Ow, ow, ow!" barked Alice.

Iantha had finished her fish. She started to pull the bathing suit down again; changed her mind, pulled it off over her head, rolled it up, and threw it across the pool. Halfway across it unfolded and floated down onto the water. The mermaid then cleared her throat, took a deep breath, and, in a clear ringing soprano, launched into the heart-wrenching strains of:

> *"Rheingold!*
> *Reines Gold,*
> *Wie lauter und hell*
> *Leuchtest hold du uns!*
> *Um dich, du klares—"*

"Iantha!"

"What is it, Markee?" she giggled.

"I said, it's getting time to go home!"

"Oh, but I do not want to go home. I am having much fun.

> *"Nun wir klagen!*
> *Gebt uns das Gold—"*

"No, really, Iantha, we've got to go." He laid a hand on her shoulder. The touch made his blood tingle. At the same time, it was plain that the remains of Iantha's carefully husbanded sobriety had gone. That last race in fresh water had been like three oversized Manhattans. Through Vining's head ran a paraphrase of an old song:

> *"What shall we do with a drunken mermaid*
> *At three o'clock in the morning?"*

"Oh, Markee, always you are so serious when people are 'aving fun. But if you say please I will come."

"Very well, please come. Here, put your arm around my neck, and I'll carry you to your chair."

Such, indeed was Mark Vining's intention. He got one hand around her waist and another under her tail. Then he tried to straighten up. He had forgotten that Iantha's tail was a good deal heavier than it looked. In fact, that long and powerful structure of bone, muscle, and cartilage ran the mermaid's total weight up to the surprising figure of over two hundred and fifty pounds. The result of his attempt was to send himself and his burden headlong into the pool. To the spectators it looked as though he had picked Iantha up and then deliberately dived in with her.

He came up and shook the water out of his head. Iantha popped up in front of him.

"So!" she gurgled. "You are 'aving fun with Iantha! I think you are serious, but you want to play games! All right, I show you!" She brought her palm down smartly, filling Vining's mouth and nose with water. He struck out blindly for the edge of the pool. He was a powerful swimmer, but his street clothes hampered him. Another splash cascaded over his luckless head. He got his eyes clear in time to see Iantha's head go down and her flukes up.

"Markeeee!" The voice was behind him. He turned,

and saw Iantha holding a large black block of soft rubber. This object was a plaything for users of the Hotel Creston's pool, and it had been left lying on the bottom during the meet.

"Catch!" cried Iantha gaily, and let drive. The block took Vining neatly between the eyes.

The next thing he knew, he was lying on the wet concrete. He sat up and sneezed. His head seemed to be full of ammonia. Louis Connaught put away the smelling-salts bottle, and Laird shoved a glass containing a snort of whiskey at him. Beside him was Iantha, sitting on her curled tail. She was actually crying.

"Oh, Markee, you are not dead? You are all right? Oh, I am so sorry! I did not mean to 'it you."

"I'm all right, I guess," he said thickly. "Just an accident. Don't worry."

"Oh, I am so glad!" She grabbed his neck and gave it a hug that made its vertebrae creak alarmingly.

"Now," he said, "if I could dry out my clothes. Louie, could you—uh—"

"Sure," said Connaught, helping him up. "We'll put your clothes on the radiator in the men's shower room, and I can lend you a pair of pants and a sweatshirt while they're drying."

When Vining came out in his borrowed garments, he had to push his way through the throng that crowded the starting end of the pool room. He was relieved to note that Alice had disappeared. In the crowd, Iantha was holding court in her wheel chair. In front of her stood a large man in a dinner jacket and a black cloak, with his back to the pool.

"Permit me," he was saying. "I am Joseph Clement. Under my management, nothing you wished in the way of a dramatic or musical career would be beyond you. I heard you sing, and I know that with but little training, even the doors of the Metropolitan would fly open at your approach."

"No, Mr. Clement. It would be nice, but tomorrow I 'ave to leave for 'ome." She giggled.

"But my dear Miss Delfoiros—where is your home, if I may presume to ask?"

"Cyprus."

"Cyprus? Hm-m-m—let's see, where's that?"

"You do not know where Cyprus is? You are not a nice man. I do not like you. Go away."

"Oh, but my dear, dear Miss Del—"

"Go away, I said. Scram."

"But—"

Iantha's tail came up and lashed out, catching the cloaked man in the solar plexus.

Little Miss Havranek looked at her teammate Miss Tufts, as she prepared to make her third rescue of the evening. "Poisonally," she said, "I am getting damn sick of pulling dopes out of this pool."

The sky was just turning gray the next morning when Laird drove his huge old limousine out into the driveway of his house in the Bronx. The wind was driving a heavy rain almost horizontally.

He got out and helped Vining carry Iantha into the car. Vining got in the back with the mermaid. He spoke into the voice tube: "Jones Beach, Chauncey."

"Aye, aye, sir," came the reply. "Listen, Mark, you sure we remembered everything?"

"I made a list and checked it." He yawned. "I could have done with some more sleep last night. Are you sure you won't fall asleep at the wheel?"

"Listen, Mark, with all the coffee I got sloshing around in me, I won't get to sleep for a week."

"We certainly picked a nice time to leave."

"I know we did. In a coupla hours, the place'll be covered six deep with reporters. If it weren't for the weather, they might be arriving now. When they do, they'll find the horse has stolen the stable door—that isn't what I mean, but you get the idea. Listen, you better pull down some of those curtains until we get out on Long Island."

"Righto, Herb."

Iantha spoke up in a small voice. "Was I very bad last night when I was drunk, Mark?"

"Not very. At least, not worse than I'd be if I went swimming in a tank of sherry."

"I am so sorry—always I try to be nice, but the fresh water gets me out of my head. And that poor Mr. Clement, that I pushed in the water—"

"Oh, he's used to temperamental people. That's his business. But I don't know that it was such a good idea on the way home to stick your tail out of the car and biff that cop under the chin with it."

She giggled. "But he looked so surprised!"

"I'll say he did! But a surprised cop is sometimes a tough customer."

"Will that make trouble for you?"

"I don't think so. If he's a wise cop, he won't report it at all. You know how the report would read: 'Attacked by mermaid at corner Broadway and Ninety-eighth Street, 11:45 P.M.' And *where* did you learn the unexpurgated version of 'Barnacle Bill the Sailor'?"

"A Greek sponge diver I met in Florida told me. 'E is a friend of us mer-folk, and he taught me my first English. 'E used to joke me about my Cypriot accent when we talked Greek. It is a pretty song, is it not?"

"I don't think 'pretty' is exactly the word I'd use."

" ''Oo won the meet? I never did 'ear."

"Oh, Louie and Herb talked it over, and decided they'd both get so much publicity out of it that it didn't much matter. They're leaving it up to the A. A. U., who will get a first-class headache. For instance, we'll claim we didn't foul Alice, because Louie had already disqualified her by his calling and fish-waving. You see that's coaching, and coaching a competitor during an event is illegal.

"But look here, Iantha, why do you have to leave so abruptly?"

She shrugged. "My business with 'Erbert is over, and I promised to be back to Cyprus for my sister's baby being born."

"You don't lay eggs? But of course you don't. Didn't I just prove last night you were mammals?"

"Markee, what an idea! Anyway, I do not want to stay around. I like you and I like 'Erbert, but I do not like living on land. You just imagine living in water for yourself, and you get an idea. And if I stay, the newspapers come, and soon all New York knows about me. We merfolk do not believe in letting the land men know about us."

"Why?"

"We used to be friends with them sometimes, and always it made trouble. And now they 'ave guns and go around shooting things a mile away, to collect them, my great-uncle was shot in the tail last year by some aviator man who thought he was a porpoise or something. We don't like being collected. So when we see a boat or an airplane coming, we duck down and swim away quick."

"I suppose," said Vining slowly, "that that's why there were plenty of reports of mer-folk up to a few centuries ago, and then they stopped, so that now people don't believe they exist."

"Yes. We are smart, and we can see as far as the land

men can. So you do not catch us very often. That is why
this business with 'Erbert, to buy ten thousand bathing
caps for the mer-folk, 'as to be secret. Not even his company will know about it. But they will not care if they
get their money. And we shall not 'ave to sit on rocks
drying our 'air so much. Maybe later we can arrange to
buy some good knives and spears the same way. They
would be better than the shell things we use now."

"I suppose you get all these old coins out of wrecks?"

"Yes. I know of one just off—no, I must not tell you.
If the land men know about a wreck, they come with
divers. Of course, the very deep ones we do not care
about, because we cannot dive down that far. We 'ave to
come up for air, like a whale."

"How did Herb happen to suck you in on that swimming meet?"

"Oh, I promised him when he asked—when I did not
know 'ow much what-you-call-it fuss there would be.
When I found out, he would not let me go back on my
promise. I think he 'as a conscience about that, and that
is why he gave me that nice fish spear."

"Do you ever expect to get back this way?"

"No, I do not think so. We 'ad a committee to see
about the caps, and they chose me to represent them. But
now that is arranged, and there is no more reason for me
going out on land again."

He was silent for a while. Then he burst out: "Damn it
all, Iantha, I just can't believe that you're starting off this
morning to swim the Atlantic, and I'll never see you
again."

She patted his hand. "Maybe you cannot, but that is
so. Remember, friendships between my folk and yours always make people un'appy. I shall remember you a long
time, but that is all there will ever be to it."

He growled something in his throat, looking straight in
front of him.

She said: "Mark, you know I like you, and I think you like me. 'Erbert 'as a moving-picture machine in his house, and he showed me some pictures of 'ow the land folk live.

"These pictures showed a custom of the people in this country, when they like each other. It is called—kissing, I think. I should like to learn that custom."

"Huh? You mean *me?*" To a man of Vining's temperament, the shock was almost physically painful. But her arms were already sliding around his neck. Presently twenty firecrackers, six Roman candles, and a skyrocket seemed to go off inside him.

"Here we are, folks," called Laird. Getting no response, he repeated the statement more loudly. A faint and un-enthusiastic "Yeah" came through the voice tube.

Jones Beach was bleak under the lowering March clouds. The wind drove the rain against the car windows.

They drove down the beach road a way, till the tall tower was lost in the rain. Nobody was in sight.

The men carried Iantha down on the beach and brought the things she was taking. These consisted of a boxful of cans of sardines, with a strap to go over the shoulders; a similar but smaller container with her personal belongings, and the fish spear, with which she might be able to pick up lunch on the way.

Iantha peeled off her land-woman's clothes and pulled on the emerald bathing cap. Vining, watching her with the skirt of his overcoat whipping about his legs, felt as if his heart was running out of his damp shoes onto the sand.

They shook hands, and Iantha kissed them both. She squirmed down the sand and into the water. Then she was gone. Vining thought he saw her wave back from the crest of a wave, but in that visibility he couldn't be sure.

They walked back to the car, squinting against the drops. Laird said: "Listen, Mark, you look as if you'd just taken a right to the button."

Vining merely grunted. He had gotten in front with Laird and was drying his glasses with his handkerchief, as if that were an important and delicate operation.

"Don't tell me you're hooked?"

"So what?"

"Well, I suppose you know there's absolutely nothing you can do about it."

"Herb!" Vining snapped angrily. "Do you have to point out the obvious?"

Laird, sympathizing with his friend's feelings, did not take offense. After they had driven a while, Vining spoke on his own initiative. "That," he said, "is the only woman I've ever known that made me feel at ease. I could talk to her."

Later, he said, "I never felt so damn mixed up in my life. I doubt whether anybody else ever did, either. Maybe I ought to feel relieved it's over. But I don't."

Pause. Then: "You'll drop me in Manhattan on your way back, won't you?"

"Sure, anywhere you say. Your apartment?"

"Anywhere near Times Square will do. There's a bar there I like."

So, thought Laird, at least the normal male's instincts were functioning correctly in the crisis.

THE GHOSTS
OF MELVIN PYE

There it was again.

Bernard Rigoulot heaved himself up on one elbow, staring into the darkness.

He told himself, Don't be a fool, Barney. It's your imagination. There ain't no such things—it's your imagination. You're getting old—ought to go to a doctor. If you can't afford a doctor, a clinic then!

The argument between two persons murmured and twittered along the floor and up the wall.

Rigoulot thought, If they're going to keep me awake, they might talk so as I can hear them.

The argument waxed suddenly, like a radio turned up.

"You scoundrel, he's awake," said one voice.

"I know, buddy," said the second voice.

"You'll scare him!"

"That's what I wanna do."

"It's against the rules." Here came a vulgar noise made with the mouth. Then an apparition appeared.

It was the wraith of a stout, dark man of forty, with a small mustache, and dressed in a neatly pressed, double-breasted dark suit. It leaned over the foot of the bed, extended a plump forefinger, and said:

"Boo!"

Rigoulot poked his wife. "Hey, honey! Wake up!"

Bertha awoke. "What is it?"

"Looky there! Do you see what I see?"

"Looks like a ghost," she said.

"I *am* a ghost!" the wraith said. "Heh-heh-heh!"

"Eeeeek!" said Mrs. Rigoulot, and pulled the covers over her head.

"Heh-heh," continued the ghost. "That's showing 'em, Phony, old boy?"

"Will you stop?" said a voice—either the same voice or another identical with it. At that point, Rigoulot, too, pulled the covers over his head.

The Conroy Realty Company—in private life George Conroy—looked up from its desk with a forced smile, knowing that tenants called only about complaints.

"Hello, Mr. Conroy," said Bernard Rigoulot.

"Hello, Mr.—uh—Rigoulot," said Conroy. "I'll have a man over to fix that burner in a couple of days."

Rigoulot ignored that remark. "I aim to break my lease," he said.

"You can't do that! A lease is a contract. I'll have that oil burner fixed!"

" 'Tain't that. It's ha'nts."

"Ants? I'll get the exterminator."

"Ha'nts, not ants. Ghosts—things that go *woooo*."

"You're crazy, man."

Rigoulot shook his head.

"I seen what I seen, and so did my wife," he said. "Yesterday my hands was shaking so I couldn't draw. So I'm leaving unless you can get rid of the ha'nts."

"Now Mr. Rigoulot, what's the real reason you want to leave?"

"I told you. Ha'nts."

Conroy sighed. "Look. Will you stay on if I spend a night in your house and see the ghost?"

"Mebbe. If you can get rid of the ghost, I'll see."

When Rigoulot had left, Conroy spoke to his secretary.

"Mrs. Small, get out the file on that block of houses on One Hundred Seventy-Fifth Place." Then he answered the telephone.

"Yes, Mrs. Barth, I'll send a man over right away. In a couple of days. Well, next Friday at the latest."

"Better do something about that stove, Mr. Conroy," said the secretary. "The Barths are two months behind on their rent and say they won't pay until it's fixed."

"Did you send them the usual notices?"

"Yes, but they didn't weaken."

Conroy sighed. "Guess we'll have to fix their blasted stove. Find out how much it'll be."

Mrs. Small got out the file on Rigoulot's house, and Conroy studied it.

"*Unh,*" he said. "That's where that guy Pye was killed. That was before we took over the block. *Hm.*"

"Scared?" said Mrs. Small.

Before Conroy could frame a biting reply, the telephone rang again.

"It's Miss Winston," Mrs. Small said.

The Conroy Realty Company disappeared and George Conroy, the Man, took its place. He spoke into the instrument in monosyllables, half of them being *"Unh."*

"Okay, Babs, six," he ended. "By-by."

"Why don't you marry her, boss?" said Mrs. Small. "You owe it to her after monopolizing her time for ten years. Or are you afraid of dividing up your income?"

Conroy glared.

"I don't pry into your affairs, Mrs. Small!" he growled, and buried himself in the file on Rigoulot's house.

Conroy arrived at the Rigoulot house at 9 P.M. and drank the glass of beer that Rigoulot offered him. Mrs. Rigoulot excused herself and went to bed. Conroy did not miss her, for her conversation was confined to platitudes.

"You're one of my prize tenants, you know," he told Rigoulot. "Always on time with the rent. I'd hate to lose you."

"I was just brought up that way," said Rigoulot. "I don't accep' favors. But see here: I can't live in a ha'nted house. If I get so shaky I can't draw, you won't have no rent or tenant or nothing." He looked at the clock. " 'Leven fifty. Guess it's time to turn the lights out."

The time they sat in the darkness seemed longer than it actually was. Then a faint mutter trickled along the wainscoting. It drifted this way and that, growing louder. Conroy felt that his blood had left his viscera to concentrate in his scalp.

"Ga wan, scram!"

"How dare you!"

"To hell with the rules. I'm feeling good. *Whoop!*"

The apparition popped into view.

Conroy was as brave as most, and there was nothing too alarming about a plump, middle-aged ghost in a double-breasted suit. But Conroy had his share of atavistic fears. He rose, tensing his muscles to keep his knees from knocking.

"Who are you?" said Conroy.

"Heh-heh," said the ghost. "So *you're* that low-down landlord? Another mama's boy, like Phony. Watch out! Gonna getcha!" The ghost grimaced and extended clutching hands.

Conroy stood it as long as he could. Then something snapped, and he found himself outside and running. Ghostly laughter behind him made him run faster. But he did not go too fast to reflect that this phenomenon was practically certain to cost him money. . . .

The next morning, after some hesitation, Conroy worked up his courage to call the detective agency. He might never have committed himself to the expense but for Mrs. Small's sarcasms.

"Well, shall I do it for you?" she had asked.

The detective turned out to be a burly man named Edward Kalesky, who might have been left over from the Paleolithic.

"Spooks?" he said. "You wouldn't kid me, Mr. Conroy?"

"I never kid," said Conroy.

"I mean, are they real or phony?"

"That's for you to find out. It is a coincidence that a man named Melvin Pye was murdered by a burglar in that house ten years ago. All I know about him is his name, because we didn't own that block of houses then."

Kalesky approached Rigoulot's house without qualms. He was a good detective, having enough imagination to guess what other people might do but not so much as to let unusual events give him creepy-crawlies. He was a little depressed about working "way out in the sticks," by which he meant in a region where houses had lawns.

No. 10915 175th Place was a small brick house in suburban Georgian, exactly like all the other houses in the block except for details of coloring. Rigoulot, forewarned, let Kalesky in and made him comfortable.

The apparition, however, failed to appear on schedule. Instead, when midnight arrived, Kalesky's hair was raised by shrieks from next door. He started out, and met the ghost coming in.

"Whee!" said the apparition. "Got lost. All these goddam houses look alike. See, Phony?" The wraith hiccupped.

Kalesky quietly whipped out a blackjack and swung. He was not prepared to have the weapon pass through the apparition without resistance. As a result he swung himself halfway around, turned his ankle on the top step, and fell heavily.

He sat up, feeling his hurts, and groaned. Rigoulot popped into sight at the door.

"Reckon blackjacks ain't no good for ha'nts," he said.

"Ga wan, you cheap little tenant you!" snarled the ghost, making a snatch at Rigoulot, who disappeared up the stairs. The ghost looked down at Kalesky.

"A flatfoot, huh? Nosey gumshoe, coming to spoil my fun! I'll fix you! I'll follow you home, going *woooo!* I'll crawl in bed with you and rattle my teeth. I'll materialize just my head on your mantlepiece and tell your relatives what I think of them. I'll—let go, you! Scram! I don't give a hoot." The ghost seemed to be struggling with something, and gradually faded from sight.

Kalesky picked himself up and limped back to his hotel, muttering.

Next morning, Kalesky called Conroy and told him what had happened. Conroy gave him little sympathy, having troubles of his own. The tenant of 10917, which the ghost had mistakenly invaded, was also threatening to skip.

Kalesky spent the next two days examining Rigoulot's house and grounds. He had once conducted an exposé against mediums, so knew what to look for. But not a sign of a concealed loudspeaker or projector did he find. He also looked up Rigoulot. But the little tenant had a prosaic enough background. Born in South Carolina, he had worked as a draftsman in the city for twenty years.

By now Kalesky had an open mind on the subject of

the ghost of the late Melvin Pye. He got the date of the man's murder from Mrs. Small. The newspapers of that week in the public library gave some details about Pye, and the Police Department furnished Kalesky with more information. The killing had not been solved but was apparently the work of a burglar who had been surprised. Pye at that time was the treasurer of a small cafeteria chain.

Kalesky looked up the chain's offices. Most of the personnel had changed since Pye's time, but the present head of the chain had been a vice-president when Pye had worked there and remembered him.

"Yeah, he was smart as a whip," the president explained. "But I don't think he'd have gotten much further. He had a funny personality—sort of cringing. And he was so good it hurt. He didn't smoke, drink, swear, or anything. He was a good treasurer, though—careful and conscientious."

This picture of Pye did not convey an idea much like the ghost, unless the Pye character had deteriorated vastly since death. Kalesky reported to Conroy on his work.

"That's all very well," said Conroy testily. "But it doesn't get rid of the spook. Number Ten-Nine-Fifteen is vacant now."

"That little Southern guy leave?"

"Yes. He lost his job, he said, because he was too nervous to draw. Blamed me for it. He said he was moving in on some kinfolk."

"Whatcha going to do with the house?"

"I'm moving into it myself. I've been living in one of the apartments in my apartment house, but I'd have a better chance of renting the apartment than a haunted house."

"You got nerve."

"Matter of dollars, Kalesky. But what are you going to *do?*"

Thoughtfully, Kalesky rubbed his jowl.

"I dunno yet. How about my moving in with you? It would cut the expense account."

The first evening, a handsome woman, still young enough to be called a girl, rang the doorbell. When Kalesky opened it, she jumped back with a little shriek.

"Wazzamatta?" said Kalesky.

"Oh, I thought you were the ghost." She identified herself as Conroy's Miss Winston, who had come over to cook dinner for them.

Kalesky returned to his cigar and sporting page. In the kitchen he overheard Miss Winston talking.

"But George," she said, "what was I to think when the door opened and a hairy gorilla confronted me." Kalesky, who fortunately was not vain, grinned.

Miss Winston stayed to see the ghost hunt. There was not much to see. When midnight approached, Kalesky got out a camera with a photoflash attachment and put out the lights.

The argument began as usual. When the apparition popped into sight, faintly luminescent, Kalesky snapped the camera.

"Oh-oh!" said the ghost. "Getting my picture took. The real, original, authentic ghost of Melvin Pye. Beware of imitations. Hope you're having fun, flatfoot." By the time the watchers' eyes had recovered from the flash, the apparition had vanished, and the argument with the invisible interlocutor had subsided to a mumble.

Kalesky developed and printed the picture himself. It showed the living room, and in the living room the wraith, with the bookcase showing clearly through him.

"Okay," snapped Conroy. "You've proved that this house is haunted by the ghost of Melvin Pye. I knew that already. I want to get *rid* of the danged thing."

"I'm just a detective, not an ex—what are those guys that cast out devils?" said Kalesky.

"Exorcists?"

"Yeah. I'm not an exorcist. What do you expect me to do, say 'Boo!' to—say!"

When the ghost showed up that night, the closet door swung open, and a sheeted figure marched out. It stretched a bare arm toward the apparition.

"*Oooooh!*" it groaned.

"Yeow!" yelled the ghost. "I got 'em!" And he vanished.

But he instantly reappeared in another part of the room; or at least the new arrival looked like the other. "I must apologize, my dear sirs, for my double's abominable behavior," the second apparition said. "I shall take steps at the next guild meeting to have him cited for unbecoming conduct."

"Huh?" said Kalesky and Conroy together.

"I see you don't understand. I'm really the ghost of Melvin Pye. The other creature is a bogus imitation. You frightened him away so suddenly that his ectoplasm was transferred to me. Oh, dear, I do hope he doesn't go haunt the distillery again!" With which the second ghost faded out of sight.

"Hey, come back!" Kalesky called. But to no avail.

"Now what?" the detective asked Conroy.

Conroy groaned.

"We seem to have two ghosts. But the main thing still is to get rid of them. We could hire an exorcist, couldn't we?"

"I suppose so. It'd cost you more dough."

"I can stand that, I guess."

Kalesky looked up a Swami Mahananda whom he had known in his medium-busting days. The swami was a thin, dark man dressed entirely in black except for his white shirt. He was one of the few practitioners of his profession on whom Kalesky had never been able to get anything. This was why Kalesky turned to him now.

"You say," said Swami Mahananda in his high, accented voice, "that you have two ghosts, both of them claiming to be the ghost of the late Melvin Pye?"

"Uh-huh."

"That is a very peculiar case. I have heard of one other like it—the *dvirupa* mentioned in the forty-second *tantra* of Kamakrishna. I will take your case, not so much for the fee—which you understand merely covers the necessary expenses that one incurs in this materialistic land—as for the intellectual interest."

Swami Mahananda showed up at the haunted house with a large, battered suitcase. The first thing he took out of it was an orange robe, which he put on in place of his shabby black coat. He looked more impressive at once. He also unfolded a small, jointed tripod and lighted a piece of incense, which he placed therein.

"I have decided to use the old Babylonian *tabalum tatbal*," he said. "If it does not work, nothing will, for there is no more powerful exorcism." The swami set up on the mantelpiece a row of candles made in the form of demons. He unstoppered a small bottle and sprinkled water from it on a branch of a tamarisk tree.

"Now," he said, "we're ready!"

At midnight the ghost arrived with a whoop. "Whee! I'm a Bengal tiger with a toothache! I'm bad! Hear me moan? Hear my chains rattle? Nix, I haven't got any chains. Watch me drive out all this rotten landlord's tenants!"

The swami imperturbably struck a match and ignited the seven demon-candles. Then he faced the ghost and cried, waving the branch in intricate patterns:

"I raise the torch, their images I burn.
Of the *utukku,* the *shedu,* the *rabisu,* the *ekimmu,*

Of the *lilu* and *lilitu* and *ardat lili*,
And every evil that seizes hold of men!"

"Huh?" said the ghost. "Oh, hello, Giuseppe."
"Never mind my name before I was initiated," said the swami.

"Tremble, melt away, and disappear!
May your smoke rise to heaven,
May Shamash destroy your limbs, may the son of Ea
The great magician, restrain your strength!"

"Ouch," said the ghost, wavering slightly. "You play too rough." With which the ghost disappeared.

But at the same time he, or his double, reappeared.

"I'm sorry!" bleated the newcomer. "If you'll stop the exorcism a minute I'll explain."

"Well?" said the swami.

"He's been drifting over the distillery again, getting drunk on the smell. Mercy me, what a lot of stuff you have here. It's too bad it won't work on Bogus."

"Oh, yes, it will," said the swami.

"Heh-heh," said Bogus, reappearing. "That's what you think. Ga wan, Phony."

Now he was addressing another ghost. "I don't need your help to settle with this dopey wizard."

Swami Mahananda began another spell. The second ghost, Phony, faded out. Then the first ghost, Bogus, flickered from sight and the other apparition came back into view.

"Stop it, Bogus!" he cried. "You've disgraced us enough for one evening." At this point he went out again and Bogus reappeared. The changes went on for a quarter-hour—first one apparition and then the other being banished.

Finally Swami Mahananda collapsed into a chair with his head in his hands. Bogus, who happened to be visible at that instant, sneered.

"What'd I tell ya?" he gloated. "You can't exorcise the ghost of Melvin Pye. Just wait till tomorrow night; I'll have enough power then really to fix this goddam landlord!"

"Don't listen to him!" cried Phony, reappearing. "I'm the real ghost of Melvin Pye!" "You are not! I am!" The argument broke out again, and the two ghosts, still disputing, faded away.

"It is no use, gentlemen," groaned the swami. "I can banish any spirit by himself, but the *dvirupa* is too hard to—how should I say it?—get hold of. When you push one half out, you push the other half in. I go."

The swami took off his orange robe, jammed it into his suitcase, put away his other properties, clapped on his old black hat, and departed.

"Well!" said Conroy. "Now, where does that leave us?"

"Search me," said Kalesky. "I don't think you want me on this job any more."

"Don't desert me, old man!" cried Conroy. "Didn't you hear his threats? He'll scare away all my tenants and ruin me! Please stay on a couple more days! Look into Pye's history again. There ought to be a clue there somewhere."

Kalesky shrugged.

"Okay, if you want it. But I don't promise nothing."

Kalesky began his hunt early the following morning. He found Pye's sister in another suburb, and from her he got more information.

Pye had undergone a strict upbringing and had not been very happy. Twice during his mature life he had suffered complete lapses of memory. The first time, he came to himself to find that he had joined the Marines.

He had served out his enlistment and then gone back to the accounting work he had formerly followed. The second time he had come to himself in jail. As well as he could discover, he had spent the previous year drifting around as an itinerant laborer. He had landed in jail as a result of a weakness for visiting waterfronts and picking fights with sailors.

Pye's sister referred Kalesky to the psychiatrist who had treated Pye after his second break—a Dr. Ekstrom. Kalesky looked Ekstrom up in the telephone directory and went to his office.

Dr. William Ekstrom was a tall, slender man with silvery hair, who looked like an actor playing the part of a distinguished psychiatrist.

"Pye was a case of split personality," he said. "The hedonistic, adventurous aspects of his psyche, so sternly repressed in early life, collected in his subconscious to form a secondary personality. Twice this second idea-complex got the upper hand. It is as though two personalities, P-One and P-Two, were alternating in their control of one body."

"You wouldn't kid me, Doc?" Kalesky asked. "Some people can have two minds in one body?"

"Yes, my dear chap, they can. I might have been able to cure Pye if he hadn't died when he did."

"How do you cure them?"

"You merge the two personalities under hypnosis. But look here; what's all this getting at? The man's dead, you know."

"Well, Doc," said Kalesky uncomfortably, "he is and he isn't. I mean."

"Yes?"

Kalesky finally told the story. When he had finished, Ekstrom nodded.

"Fascinating, my dear friend," he said. "Here, will you

cross your knees a moment?" When Kalesky did so, Ekstrom smote him below the kneecap with a little rubber hammer. Kalesky's leg flew up.

"You don't have to worry about me being nuts," said Kalesky. "That stuffed shirt Conroy will tell you the same thing. Have you got an engagement this evening?"

"No, but—here, what have you in mind?" said Ekstrom suspiciously.

Kalesky opened his wallet and counted out five tens.

"If you could have merged him while he was alive, you can merge him when he's dead."

"Don't be silly, old man. I'm not a psychic researcher. But—" as Kalesky began to gather up the money "—it might be worth trying at that. You understand that if there's no ghost, I keep the retainer."

"We'll have to handle this carefully," Ekstrom said. "I understand that the hedonistic personality, or P-Two—the one called Bogus—is fond of alcohol. Who has a bottle of spirits?"

A bottle of whiskey was produced. Ekstrom poured the contents into the bathtub and soaked a bath towel in the liquid, to faint groans from Conroy and Kalesky. Then he hung the towel in the living room. Soon the smell made the air hardly breathable.

"Ah-hah!" cried Bogus, oozing out of the fireplace. "Now I'm really going to town on your houses, you fresh little realtor, you! When I get through you won't have a tenant. Hello, aren't you that dumb little psychiatrist who was always trying to merge me with Phony?"

"Yes," said Ekstrom.

"Well, you can go stick your head in a bucket. I don't want any part of that lousy imitation ghost."

"That's all right, old fellow," said Ekstrom heartily. "Don't you like the liquor?"

Bogus sniffed. "Say, that's not bad stuff. Mean you

fixed it up for me? Maybe I misjudged you, Doc. But no mergers with that sissy, understand!" He leaned back, as if reclining on an invisible sofa. "Hey, Phony, get a load of this!"

"Can you tell me why you ghosts wear suits instead of sheets?" Kalesky asked.

"Because we're buried in suits instead of sheets. That reminds me—aren't you the guy who came out of the closet with a sheet on and scared me out of my ecto-plasm? I'll get even with you. Right now, though, I'm feeling too good." The ghost yawned.

Ekstrom took out a pocket flashlight.

"Mr. Pye," he said. "Here's a little experiment that might interest you." He focused a spot of light on the ceiling, and moved it slowly back and forth. "Watch that spot. It's warm in here. Just the temperature for sleeping. Your eyelids are getting heavy. A feeling of numbness is stealing over you. You're falling asleep—asleep—asleep."

Five minutes of this reduced Bogus to a rigid, glassy-eyed wraith. Then the other ghost appeared.

"My goodness!" cried Phony. "What have you done to him, Doctor Ekstrom? I never thought anybody could control him, he's so wild. He pays no attention to the rules and gets away with it. Politics, you know."

"What rules?" asked Kalesky.

"Union rules, about haunting quietly and invisibly. We adopted them after so many haunted houses were torn down. It's a terrible thing to be a ghost whose house has been torn down."

"Do you have to haunt?" Conroy asked.

"Yes, sir. I was murdered here, so I have to haunt the house till my murder is avenged. But the felon who slew me is in prison for life, so I shall have to await his natural death."

"Don't getting sent up for life count as avenging a murder?" Kalesky asked.

"It would, only this burglar wasn't sentenced for murdering *me*. He killed one of his fellow-felons."

"I could have this house torn down," Conroy said thoughtfully.

"Deary me," said Phony. "You wouldn't do that, sir?"

"If I couldn't stop the haunting otherwise."

"But it wouldn't do any good. All the other houses in the block are built to the same plan as this. Practically speaking they *are* the same as this. So we'd have to haunt one of the others."

"You could tear down all the houses in the block," Kalesky said.

"Ow! Do you know what it costs to build, with crooked contractors and lazy workmen?" Conroy moaned. "It would ruin me! They're practically new, too; only twenty years old."

"I see your point of view, sir," said the ghost. "I wish I could help—"

"You can," broke in Ekstrom. "All we have to do is merge you with Bogus. The combined ghost would be a fine, well-balanced character who wouldn't give any trouble."

"What, merge me with that uncouth buffoon?" shrieked Phony, fluttering his transparent hands. "Horrors! A thousand times no!"

"Aw, come on!" wheedled Kalesky. "It won't be so bad."

"You want to do the right thing, don't you?" said Conroy.

"Trust me to know best, old chap," said Ekstrom.

After a prolonged argument, the ghost gave in. "Hurry and get the horrid business over with," it wailed. "To think of my being submerged in that crass boor whom I despise!"

Ekstrom got to work with his flashlight, and soon had Phony stiff and stark like his twin. Then the psychiatrist said:

"You and Bogus are really parts of the same man. You must merge yourself with him. Each of you has virtues that the other lacks. You're only half a ghost as you are. Phony, go merge yourself with Bogus, to make a complete Melvin Pye."

Phony drifted dreamily over to where his double sprawled. He moved into the same position in the same place, whereupon there was but one ghost to be seen.

"Wake up, Melvin Pye!" cried Ekstrom.

The ghost of Melvin Pye awoke.

"Say, that's quite a trick, Doctor Ekstrom," he said, with a grin. "I remember everything that either of my former selves did."

The ghost stood up. He seemed a little larger and more substantial than either of his former components.

"Ha," he said. "Wish I'd been this way before. No telling what I'd have accomplished."

This was neither Melvin Pye, the mama's boy, nor Melvin Pye, the irresponsible roughneck. It was Melvin Pye the Man of Destiny.

"But I can still accomplish a thing or two. You! You're that tightwad landlord, aren't you?"

"I—" began Conroy.

"Shut up! You know I can empty your houses just like *that,* don't you?"

"I—"

"Shut up! From now on you'll do as I say."

"I'll get the swami—"

The ghost scowled.

"Shut up! I know enough about Giuseppe. He won't dare bother me. First, you've been letting these houses run down disgracefully. You'll have three oil burners, two stoves, six refrigerators, and four plumbing systems in this block fixed, and no slipshod job either!"

"But—"

"Will you do as I say, or must I get tough?" snarled the ghost.

"Okay. But I—"

"Shut up! Then there's that tenant who used to live here, Rigoulot. He lost his job. You'll give him one."

"But I don't need a full-time draftsman!"

"Shut up! Then there's that Miss Winston who comes around to cook dinner for you. She loves you, God knows why. Marry her."

"What?"

"You heard me! No excuses, unless you want to have to tear down all your houses. I'll be back tomorrow, to see how you're doing. I'll have thought of some more tasks by then. Good night, gentlemen." The ghost bowed briskly to Kalesky and Ekstrom, and vanished.

After a few seconds of silence, Ekstrom spoke.

"A very interesting experiment, gentlemen. The final result wasn't quite what I anticipated. I thought the united Pye would combine the timidity of Phony with the stupidity of Bogus and be easy to handle. Instead he combined the intelligence and moral fervor of Phony with the aggressive belligerence of Bogus. So you'll have to play ball with him, old man—ha-ha—unless you want to lose your houses."

Conroy made a choked sound. Ekstrom got up and looked at his watch.

"Ho-hum! I can just make the train back to town. A most interesting evening, gentlemen. I wish I dared write it up for the journals. Conroy, old fellow, where shall I send my bill? Your office—why, what are you looking at me like that for? You can't threaten me! Don't you dare touch me, Conroy! Kalesky, stop him! Help! *Ouch!*"

Seconds later, a tall, silver-haired man sprinted along the dark streets, while after him pounded, with clutching hand and bloodshot eye, the blocky figure of George Conroy. Ekstrom ran faster than Conroy—or the suburb would have had on its hands another ghost, doomed to haunt the site of its murder until suitably avenged.

THE WISDOM
OF THE EAST

Alan Bennett took a quick look up and down Fifty-Ninth Street to make sure that no acquaintance was in sight, and ducked into the elderly building.

Inside the doors was a vestibule before you started up the creaking steps. Around the vestibule were glass frames. One of these held samples of a commercial photographer's art. Another contained a brown-tinted photograph of a dark-skinned man with a prominent nose and large, liquid black eyes. Under the photograph were the words "Shri Motilal Bhulojna. Third Floor."

As Bennett stood with his back to the big glass door, absorbing this information, a voice at his elbow said: "You are Mr. Bennett, are you not?"

Bennett spun and faced Shri Motilal Bhulojna himself, in a white suit.

"Why . . . uh . . . yes," said Bennett.

"A commercial artist?"

"Yes." Bennett wondered how the fellow knew that. Of course, it is not too difficult to discover a man's occupation if you want to go to the trouble.

The Yogi was not quite so tall and thin as Bennett. He looked just about Bennett's age, which was thirty-

five, although Bennett looked older than that because his
hair had begun to gray.

"I stepped out for a minute," continued Shri Motilal.
"Will you come up? I am about to give my introductory
talk." He trotted up the creaking stairs, and Bennett followed with a slight frown of perplexity.

Halfway up, Alan Bennett figured out what was wrong.
The big glass doors opened inward. He had been standing with his back to them. To enter by those doors, it
would have been necessary to push him, Bennett, out of
the way. There were no other doors opening off the
ground-floor vestibule.

Bennett, being an artist, was not too long on logic. But
he could see that either (a) things were not what they
seemed, or (b) Shri Motilal Bhulojna had either come
down from the ceiling, or popped out of a trapdoor like
the Devil in "Faust," or had wafted through the solid
matter inclosing the vestibule.

He quickened his step. Before, he had been on the
verge of calling off his visit to the alleged Yogi. Now
nothing short of superior force would have kept him
away.

When they reached the third floor, Shri Motilal opened
a door in the conventional manner and waved Bennett
through. He said: "Will you sit there, please?"

Bennett saw a number of chairs at one side of the
room. Four of these were occupied, by one small, bleary
old man and three women: one matron built on battle-
ship lines, one middle-aged desiccated virgin, and one
blonde, square-jawed girl, good-looking but verging on
spinsterhood.

Shri Motilal Bhulojna reappeared. He still wore his
white suit but had changed his shoes for slippers and
covered his blue-black hair with a turban.

He began his lecture without hesitation, using the

British pronunciation with a slight but pervasive nasal accent and a tendency to stress the wrong syllable of a word. "My friends, before you *be*-gin a course of instruction in the discipline of Yoga, it will be desirable to clear up any misconceptions that your Western minds may be harboring.

"To begin with, it is a great *mis*-take to suppose that the mere fact of Eastern origin is any guarantee of mysterious or occult powers. India has developed her own schools of materialist philosophy. For instans, the Vaiseshika school anticipated many of your Western doctrines of atomic physics. And it is a notorious fact that India has produced her share of charlatans and fakers.

"I will not make exaggerated claims for the benefits that you will derive from the discipline of Yoga. As one of your own prophets remarked, many are called but few are chosen. Not all of you are equipped in this incarnation to achieve the state of superconsciousnes known as *samadhi,* which is the goal of our philosophy. But as you persevere you will achieve, and as you achieve you will be rewarded.

"The first branch of Yoga we shall take up is the Hatha, or physical, Yoga, for you must obviously learn to control your bodies before you can dispense with them. Later we shall work up to the Jnara or intellectual Yoga—"

Alan Bennett found that the singsong cadence of the voice was putting him to sleep. He woke up with a jerk. Shri Motilal Bhulojna noticed and looked severe. Bennett pulled himself together in time to absorb the instructions for the first two steps.

One step was abstinence. Bennett did not think he would miss the liquor much, since he was a very sparing drinker. The meatless diet did not appeal, but he supposed he could put up with it for a while anyway. The ban on smoking promised to be a real hardship.

The other step was a preliminary bout of *dharana* or fixed attention. The five aspirants were simply to sit absolutely still for one hour. Having issued that instruction, Shri Motilal kicked off his slippers, hitched up his white pants, sat down on the floor, and settled himself in the lotus posture, with each foot resting on the opposite thigh. Then to all appearances he became a brown-skinned statue.

At the end of ten minutes, Alan Bennett developed an itch on his nose, then an itch in his left foot, then an itch on his right shoulder blade. The itches spread until Alan Bennett was one vast itch.

At twenty-five minutes, the bleary little man coughed loudly, got up, and walked out muttering, "Damn foolishness." Bennett sympathized with him but did not intend to leave until he had settled the question of how a man can go through a glass door without opening it. The incident took Bennett's mind off his itches for a while, although they soon returned.

When they seemed utterly intolerable, Shri Motilal uncoiled himself, got up, and said: "That will be all, friends. I trust I shall see you tomorrow night at the same time. Good night."

Bennett had his mouth half open to ask about the door, but he lacked the brass to force the question on the Yogi in the face of such a plain implication to depart.

Bennett had trouble with his pictures the next day. He blamed it on the landlady's noise, on the humidity, on the poorness of the light coming through the skylights of his studio—it was a summer-thunder-showery day—and finally on the real cause, which was his curiosity about the incident of the glass doors.

He arrived at Bhulojna's nearly half an hour early, which would have sounded fantastic to those who knew Alan Bennett's habits. He was the first to appear. Bhulojna told him to make himself comfortable and floated off into some inner sanctum.

Then the blonde arrived. She said: "Hello. I'm Pauline Edge. Your name's Bennett, isn't it?"

Bennett admitted with some reluctance that it was.

The girl continued: "Mother's running some club thingummy tonight, but she told me to come and remember everything Mr. Bhulojna said." They talked about the weather, discovered that they had a couple of acquaintances in common, and in a few minutes were old friends.

Bennett said: "What do you do, Pauline?"

"Me? I just puppy-dog mother."

"Is that your idea of fun?"

"Lord, no. But I'm not fitted to do anything else. We're members of the New Poor, you know. Have been for ten years. I'm not pretty enough for modeling. I'd have at least learned to run a typewriter, but mother wouldn't have it, and since she has what little money there is, here I am. That's what comes of being raised to be a debutante, damn it!"

"How'd you happen in here?"

"Some more of mother's ideas. Now that she's paid for the course, at least one of us will have to go through with it. How about you?"

"Me?" said Bennett. "Oh, I don't know. I was getting bored with my friends, and I thought I ought to have some interests besides my pictures. So I thought I'd see what there was to this wisdom-of-the-East idea."

"Here comes the Master now," said Pauline.

Shri Motilal Bhulojna drifted in. "Good evening, friends," he said, blandly unconcerned with the shrinkage in his audience. "Tonight I give you some more of the ideological background of Yoga, so that you shall understand that it is not hocus-pocus. We can be more informal now that the materialists have fallen by the wayside, as they always do.

"The postures of Hatha-Yoga, known as *asana,* are the means of raising the transcendental elements in your personalities to their rightful position of control over the material elements. By ascending the triad of *dharana, dhyana* and *samadhi,* you not only gain command of your own bodies—including the so-called 'involuntary' functions—but over the forces of nature, and eventually achieve unity with the universal spirit—"

At this point Bennett began to lose the thread of the argument. He could not decide whether he was stupid not to understand all these metaphysical terms, or whether Bhulojna was putting something over on him.

He wished most avidly for a smoke. He interrupted the flow of metaphysics to ask: "Excuse me, but how long do I have to give up these things—smoking and drinking and such?"

Shri Motilal looked at him pityingly. "These things are merely the first items on the list of things you will give up."

"Huh? You mean there's more?"

"That is so. Of course, since neither of you is married, it is unnecessary for me even to mention one of the subjects."

Pauline Edge here gave a gurgle of suppressed laughter, whereat the Yogi looked very stern indeed. "I see nothing humorous in such a matter, Miss Edge. You do not appear to realize the sacrifice I am making by offering myself as your *guru.* To live in this den of materialism; to degrade myself by accepting *money*— But then, how could you? You cannot know how you handicap me in my mastery of the highest grade of Yoga—the Yoga of Patanjali, the Yoga of inaction—for you have never experienced it. The fault is mine. I should have told you that as you advans in your studies, you will miss these material pleasures less and less. If you attain *samadhi,* your attitude toward material things will be one of indifference or even disgust."

Bennett asked: "What's the purpose of that?"

"Ah, that is the whole point. It is hard to explain the unexplainable, but I will try. Buddhism, which is in a sense a heretical offshoot of Yoga, expresses it thus: the five aggregates of grasping are pain. The cause of pain is the craving that leads to rebirth. The cessation of pain depends on the cessation of craving, which is attained by the disintegration of the aggregates that compose the personality. Our doctrine is slightly different from that, but it gives you an idea—" And Shri Motilal was off again, his fingers making delicate patterns in the air and his eyes fixed on something far away.

"Now," he said, "let us try the lotus posture. It would be unwise for you to assume it more than fifteen minutes of material time on the first trial. Remove your shoes."

Pauline had no great difficulty in getting into the position. Bennett accomplished it only after much painful grunting and cracking of joints. Bhulojna said: "No, do not place your right hand on your knee. That is the heretical Buddhist variant." And he floated off.

After a few minutes of silence, a grunt came from Alan Bennett. Then an indescribable sound that, if he had not been trying to maintain a meditative silence, would have been, "For God's sake get me out of this!"

He made a few movements to try to escape from the posture, but they did no good. He was stuck. He felt like a rat in a trap, and the fact that the trap was composed of his own members only made the sensation the more gruesome. He tugged and pushed at his feet, but that only aggravated the pain.

Pauline looked at him, then cried in alarm: "Help! Mr. Bhulojna!"

The Yogi drifted through the solid wall of the room. While Bennett forgot his agony and Pauline gawped, Shri

Motilal touched a couple of Bennett's muscles. Bennett's legs came out of their contortion.

Bennett said: "How . . . how did you do that?"

"How did I— Ah, you mean my entrance. I told you that we attain to control over the forces of nature."

"Is that how you came through the door last night?"

"Yes. I fear I grow careless. You have cost me a severe setback, for the essence of these powers is that one shall be too indifferent to the material world to use them. Can you rise?"

Bennett tried. The other two finally got him to his feet, but he could not stand anywhere near straight.

Pauline supported Alan Bennett down the stairs and out. She asked him anxiously: "How are you feeling, Alan?"

"I think my back's busted," replied Bennett.

"Oh, you poor boy! You need someone to take care of you!"

"Thanks," said Bennett, "but right now I need a drink more."

"Swell idea. But—how about Mr. Bhulojna's rules of abstinence?"

"To hell with Mr. Bhulojna."

"Still, Alan, I think he's really got something there, with his oozing through walls."

"Maybe he has. But he can keep it as far as I'm concerned. I'm an artist, not a committee for psychical research. Now how about that drink?"

By the following evening, Bennett found himself able to walk almost normally. Pauline telephoned him: "Alan, are you still interested in the wisdom of the East?"

"*No!* Well, maybe I am a little, but not to the extent of tying myself in hard knots for it. Why, Polly?"

"I think I've found one who won't tie you in knots."

"Found one what? Another Yogi?"

"Not exactly. This one calls himself a Vedantist philosopher. Name's Shri Ramanuja Bhamkh. He guarantees to give you all the Eastern wisdom you want without contortions or breathing exercises. Want to try him out?"

Bennett did.

Shri Ramanuja Bhamkh hung out on East Fifty-Ninth Street only a couple of blocks from Shri Motilal Bhulojna's place. Shri Ramanuja Bhamkh himself was a more colorful person than the Yogi—tall and powerfully built, with a long, gray beard and bushy eyebrows. His audience was much the same sort of crowd that Bennett had found at Bhulojna's the first time, only bigger.

Bennett had been late, in accordance with his usual habits. He arrived when Bhamkh was saying: "—wherefore the self is not the unity of the evergrowing and changing mental experiences. The self in dreamless sleep cannot satisfy our need, since it is empty of all content and is a bare abstraction. The true self is the universal consciousness existing both in and for itself. The three states of the soul—waking, dreaming, and sleeping—are included in a fourth—*turiya*—which is intuitional consciousness, where there is no knowledge of objects internal or external. It is the unchanged and persistent identity which continues in the midst of all change—"

Bennett did not understand this, but his artist's sense could appreciate the fine picture that Shri Ramanuja made with his turban and beard and sweeping arms.

"—which brings us the doctrine of *Maya,* the world illusion. Every object tends to pass away from itself to something else. The categories of time, space, and cause, which bind experience, are self-contradictory. Our knowledge of the world is inconsistent—"

"Wonder if I could get him to pose for me," thought Bennett. "They wanted a rajah for that blended-rye ad—"

After it was all over, Bennett said to his friend: "I didn't quite get it all, I'm afraid."

"Neither did I," replied Pauline. "But isn't he picturesque? I think I'll go to the rest of the lectures in this course; they're cheap enough."

She went, and Bennett, whose own girl friends had all married or moved away a couple of years previously, went, too. By the third lecture he was getting restless.

When the audience was breaking up after Bennett's third lecture, and the usual knot was plying Shri Ramanuja with questions of honest puzzlement or spurious erudition, Bennett said to Pauline in a low voice: "Polly, all I get is words, words, and more words. Don't you think we could get more wisdom of the East for our money out of somebody else?"

Pauline looked uncomfortable. Before she answered, Shri Ramanuja Bhamkh was upon them. "My friends!" he said heartily. "I have had my spiritual eye on you for some time." Then, in a much lower voice: "How would you like to join our Inner Circle?"

"Is there one?" asked Bennett.

"Yes, surely. One does not expose the tender minds of children like these to the ancient wisdom without preparation."

Bennett queried: "Does that mean giving up all the material pleasures?"

"No, no, no silly asceticism. We merely penetrate to the reality that underlies the world illusion. Come, I beg of you."

They went.

There were three other members of the Inner Circle. All, to Bennett's surprise, were good-looking girls.

The room was dark and high-ceilinged. At the far end

was a little statue of something with a lot of arms, illuminated by a concealed red light.

Shri Ramanuja had changed to a long gown. He said solemnly: "In this, the five thousand and forty-third year of the Kali Yoga, we have gathered in the name of Ardha-narissa, to symbolize the union of the *Maya* or cosmic illusion with the *Prakriti* or plastic matter, and thereby to penetrate to the primary source of mundane things." Here followed several metaphysical sentences that Bennett understood not at all. He felt vaguely uneasy.

Bhamkh continued: "The first *mantra* or word of power that we shall learn this evening is ---." At the end of this sentence Bhamkh rounded his lips as if he were saying "oh," but no sound came forth.

"Beg pardon?" said Bennett

Bhamkh smiled. "I forgot that you are a little behind the rest of us. Know that *mantras,* which the foolish Yogis misuse as a mere hypnotic device, are in reality ideal, inaudible sounds constituting one aspect of the universe. When written, they form a universal terminology. Do you speak French?"

"A . . . a little," said Bennett, flustered.

"Know, then, that the *mantra* ---, if sounded, would be a vowel like that in the French word *bon*—an *onh* sound, It is one of the most powerful *mantras,* representing as it does the triple constitution of the cosmos. The component parts, ah, oo, mm, represent respectively the Absolute, the Relative and the relation between them. Now, say ---."

"---," mouthed Bennett.

Shri Ramanuja smiled. "With a little practice, you will be perfect. These are the defensive *mantras;* only to advanced students do I reveal the offensive ones. The next word of power is ----------."

"Huh?" said Bennett.

"----------," Bhamkh politely did not say. "It is spelled

A-v-e-l-o-k-i-t-e-s-h-v-a-r-a, and *if* it were pronounced it would be Avelokiteshvara. Say ----------."

"----------" repeated the students.

Bhamkh explained: "The *mantra* -------- assures that, should you meet with a fatal accident in the practice of your brotherhood, you will be reborn at one of the ten points of space."

He continued to instruct his class in ideal, inaudible sounds. Bennett found it harder and harder to keep his faculties with him. He was not exactly sleepy, but his mind seemed bent on wrapping itself into a fuzzy, trance-like state.

Bennett tried to concentrate on Bhamkh's instructions, but that only made it worse. He tried the multiplication table, but that did no good. He was not alarmed; merely curious and a little peeved, as he was when he found himself to have drunk beyond his modest capacity, that his mind would no longer behave as he wished it to.

The thought drifted through his mind again: what a swell picture the old guy would make! At once the mists cleared a little. Bennett, with the still-conscious part of his mind, felt relief. If it was as easy to escape as that, there was nothing to worry about. He let himself slip a little further into the trance again. He noted with lack of much interest that the four girls were all leaning forward with glassy eyes.

Shri Ramanuja Bhamkh straightened up. "Enough instruction," he said. "We are now ready for the climax of our meeting; the consummation of our contact with the reality of which the world illusion is but the shadow; the worship of the female creative principle!"

That brought the tiny, still-conscious fragment of Bennett's mind up standing. Whatever worship of the female creative principle was, Alan Bennett did not like the sound of it.

But it was so hard to think, and his body refused utterly to obey the feeble commands of that two per cent of a mind . . .

Bhamkh looked the audience over, ending with Pauline Edge. "You," he breathed, "as the newest member of our circle, shall officiate this time!"

Bennett frantically turned on his knowledge of art. The lighting and composition would make a swell magazine cover—

Slowly his mind came awake, feeling for all the world like an arm to which the circulation is returning after having been cut off.

Bennett pushed himself out of his chair, inch by inch. He croaked "J-j-just a m-m-minute—"

Shri Ramanuja whirled. "What is this? You interrupt the Master?" He took two steps forward and did not say the *mantra* "----- ----- --!"

Bennett reeled backward as from a blow. Bhamkh followed.

"------!"

Bennett felt the floor leave his feet.

"--- ----- -- --------!" A great wind whipped at Bennett's bony form. He slid toward the door, faster and faster, down the stairs, and through the glass doors at the entrance to the building. He went through the glass, not by any mystical process, but with a loud crash and tinkle.

He picked himself up. There was a small cut on his wrist. A couple of pedestrians were looking at him. He lunged back at the doorway. As soon as he stepped inside it that wind—which did not seem to blow anything but him about—caught him, and the floor became slippery under his feet.

He gave up that attack. You needed fire to fight the Devil. And the best fire merchant lived only two blocks away.

Shri Motilal Bhulojna unwound himself and looked up at the panting Bennett when the latter burst in without knocking. The Yogi said with the faintest hint of querulousness:

"You have interrupted my concentration. Why?"

Bennett told his story.

"Ah, well," said Bhulojna. "I could have told you that Bhamkh was a secret Tantrist, and a left-hand one at that. If you had persevered in your study of Yoga to the attainment of even a fraction of my powers, you would have been able to deal with him."

"Can you?" said Bennett.

"Yes. That is, I could have up to last week."

"You mean you've forgotten how?" cried Bennett.

"Not at all. It is merely that I have mastered the Yoga of Patanjali, the great Yoga of inaction. I shall return to India and devote myself to the highest form of my philosophy, the doing of nothing."

"But . . . but—you don't want this guy Bhamkh to . . . uh . . . do whatever he's going to do?"

"I do not *want* anything. The word and all that is in it are utterly unimportant to me."

Bennett danced with frantic anxiety. "But . . . but—"

Bhulojna said thoughtfully: "There is one thing I can do. I will not thwart this Tantrist personally, as that would involve action on my part. But I will summon a fellow adept, who may be able to help you, heretical Mahayanian though he be."

Bhulojna closed his eyes. He remained absolutely still, not even breathing, for one minute, while Bennett fidgeted.

There was a glow at one side of the room. Through the wall glided a small yellow man in an extremely dirty yellow robe. He was sitting on nothing in the lotus posture.

Bhulojna said in a bored, faraway voice: "This, Alan

Bennett, is the Pan-chen-rin-po-cho, sometimes called the Tashi Lama. He already knows your story. He will help you."

"Oh, will I?" squeaked the little yellow man. "All the way from Tashilhunpo to rescue the negligible victim of an unimportant Tantrist? It shows less than your usual good sense, Shri Motilal. Anyway, I am not sure that my principles will let me."

"Why?" yelled Bennett.

"It might result in the loss of the Tantrist's life. And I am not permitted to take life under any circumstances. For instance—" He extended a plump wrist. Bennett took a good look at it; then almost fell backward in his haste to put yards between the Tashi Lama and himself. He gagged.

"You see?" said the Lama. "I must not kill one of my little six-legged friends, or even deprive it of a warm and comfortable home. So to take the life of a Tantrist would be out of the question."

Bennett asked: "Couldn't you teach me what to do? Then the blame would be mine."

"No. It would still be mine, though at second remove."

Bennett had a horrible inspiration. He shot out a skinny arm; his fingers snatched at the Lama's skin where the arthropod life clustered.

"Now," he grated, "I've got four or five of your little six-legged friends between my thumb and forefinger—"

"Murderer!" screamed the Lama. "Return my friends at once!"

"Not until I get the dope from you on how to fix Bhamkh. If you won't do it, I'll squeeze and squash—"

"All right, all right!" panted the Tashi Lama. "I will do it! To sacrifice one life to save five will not, I hope, exclude me from the ranks of the Bodhisattvas."

Bhulojna said: "You may return the Pan-chen-rin-po-

cho's guests, Alan Bennett. What he says he will do, he
will do."

That seemed plausible, in view of the Lama's fantastic
scrupulousness about killing. And Bennett had no pillbox
to keep the Lama's friends in. He obeyed.

When the transfer had been effected, the Tashi Lama
gave the impatient Bennett several *mantras*. Bennett
dashed out of the building without amenities.

Bennett bounded through the shattered door of the
building that housed Shri Ramanuja Bhamkh. The wind
caught at him and held him.

"------!" Bennett did not say. The wind ceased so suddenly that he almost fell forward.

He bounded up the stairs. When the stairs turned
slippery, Bennett did not say, "----- -----!" When his weight
disappeared, another *mantra* brought it back again.

Almost immediately, a new sound penetrated to Bennett's ears. Something, evidently in Bhamkh's studio, was
going *tweedle tweedle twee* with an air of intense self-
importance. Bhamkh seemed to have run out of, or
given up on, long-range *mantras;* the entrance to the
Inner Circle neither writhed, bit, slipped, nor displayed
undue originality. It opened.

Shri Ramanuja was doing the *tweedle-tweeing*. He was
attired as Krishna, engaged in a loose-kneed, bowlegged
dance, and breathing hard. One of the excessive number
of arms with which he appeared to be equipped was occupied in tweedling. On the floor before him, Pauline
Edge sat cross-legged with her arms up. Back of her sat
the other three girls in a similar posture. They were all
singing a hymn that was not less beautiful for the fact
that it was completely inaudible.

Bennett dashed across the room and pointed at Shri
Ramanuja. "------!"

The Tantrist reeled from the attack, but came back with one of his own: "— — —!"

"____ — — — -!" retorted Bennett.

"____!"

"___ ____ ____ —!"

"-!"

Shri Ramanuja abandoned the duel of *mantras* and tried another form of hostilities. Before Bennett's eyes he grew and changed into a towering black figure with ten arms. Each arm bore a lethal weapon. He advanced on Bennett.

But when the Tantrist changed form, the four girls at once came out of their trances. They looked at each other and then at the thing that Shri Ramanuja had become. One of them scrambled to her feet and ran out the door; one sat where she was and shrieked; one tried to bury her face in the floor boards.

Pauline Edge showed a better grasp of the situation. She picked up one of the empty chairs, climbed on another chair, and with the first chair she hit the ten-armed nightmare over its fanged, goggle-eyed head.

The chair splintered and the thing staggered. Bennett, who had with what he thought was his last breath been damning the Tashi Lama for not foreseeing this, jumped forward and wrenched a spear from one of the ten black hands. He reversed the weapon and jabbed; felt the point go in.

Then he was chasing the thing downstairs and out into Fifty-Ninth Street. It was very late, and few people were abroad. The nearest person was a citizen named Pascarella, whose trade was the robbery by force of arms of financial institutions. Mr. Pascarella, seeing ten feet of ten-armed Hindu demon bearing down on him, drew a pistol, fired once, and dropped dead of heart failure.

The thing also fell, kicked a little, and changed back

into Shri Ramanuja Bhamkh. While the crowd brought out
by the shot gathered around the corpes of the bank robber
and the man in the beard and turban, Bennett and Pauline
Edge slipped away. They found a doorway in which they
stood and simply shivered for a few minutes.

When they found their voices, Bennett said: "I suppose
we ought to go back to Bhulojna's and tell him what
happened."

Pauline nodded.

They found the Yogi in a posture more intricate than
they would have believed possible. He saw them, partly
unwound himself, and said ungraciously:

"Oh, it is you again. What is it?"

Bennett told him what had happened.

Shri Motilal mused: "Bhamkh's mistake was to resort
to material means, whereas with purely transcendental ones
he might at least have escaped with his life. He forgot that
this bizarre form he assumed would have no greater intelligence, courage, or strength of character than did the
original man. He will pay for his error by being reincar-
nated as a tapeworm, no doubt."

Bennett asked: "Is the fellow from Tibet gone? I wanted
to thank him."

"It does not matter. Such things are utterly unimportant
to him, as they are to me. I leave for India immediately."

"Oh, so soon? Polly and I were just thinking . . . uh
. . . we were a little hasty in running out on you. Would
you consider giving us some more lessons?"

"No. I have advanced to the stage where my usefulness
as a *guru* is ended, as is witnessed by my failure with you
two. Anyway, I see that you are planning a set of materialistic interests inconsistent with progress in Yoga. You
are going to ask this woman to marry you, are you not,
when you get your courage up?"

Bennett reddened, then snapped: "Yes, I am."

"Disgusting. I go." Without further farewell, Shri Moti-lal Bhulojna, still in his half-contorted posture, rose from where he coiled and drifted through the wall. He was gone.

MR. ARSON

As Clem Buckminster,, M. H. S. I. salesman for the Bronx, hung up a slightly overheated telephone, his superior cocked an eye at him and asked: "Was that the Dangerous Dane?"

Buckminster snickered dutifully. "Yeah, that was Grinnig. He's all excited about somepin. He wants me to come—"

"Does he want to shift his course again?" inquired the sales manager for the New York district.

"No; least he didn't say that. He wouldn't tell—"

"I've told you before, Clem," continued Andrews, "that this business of signing Grinnig up for a new course every month has got to stop. Let him finish one of the old ones. He's begun courses in—let me see—air conditioning, highway engineering, structural drafting, fruit growing, welding, and oil heating, and he's never gotten beyond the first lesson of any."

"But," pleaded Buckminster, "every time he finishes the first lesson, he calls me in and says, 'To hell with it. Gimme another.' 'Scuse me, Miss Cope." The last was to Andrews' secretary. "What can I do?"

"Let him slide. He's not the type that can benefit from a correspondence course."

"But I gotta earn my living. Hi, Harry!" This was to Harrison Galt, M. H. S. I. salesman for Brooklyn, who had just come in to collect the daily list of inquiries from prospective students in his district, which had been forwarded from the home office in Paterson.

Andrews continued implacably: "I know you want your half of the ten-dollar deposit. But I have specific instructions from the home office to stop signing up these lightweights who just happen to be short on sales resistance. They figured that handling their courses costs more than it's worth. Anyway, it gives the Mercury Home Study Institute a bad name."

"Anyway," sulked Buckminster, "I never signed up no Earl Browder, like one of our competitors did."

Andrews, a dryly precise man, ignored this. He asked: "What about Grinnig? Does he want to shift from oil heating to bee keeping?"

"He ain't on oil heating," said Buckminster. "He's on that new one, nigromancy."

"Huh?"

"Yeah, doncha remember? Some new idear of the School of Shop Practice. We ain't even got a folder on it, but when Grinnig seen it in one of the ads, he just had to have it. So I wrote Paterson and asked: would they please send Grinnig the first lesson booklet as soon as it was off the press."

Galt put in a word: "Speaking of the School of Shop Practice, one of my prospects told me he thought it would have to do with legal shenanigans, how to kite checks and such. Get it? He thought I meant *sharp* practice!"

"Ha, ha," said Buckminster. "The dialeck some of these guys talk, you wonder how they understand themselves. Well, so long, Mr. Andrews, I gotta—"

"Remember, Clem, no more changes of course!" interrupted Andrews. "What *is* this nigromancy course, anyway? Something to do with race relations?"

Buckminster shrugged. "I dunno. Neither did Grinnig. That's why he wanted it."

"He's crazy," said Andrews. "And so are some of the heads in Paterson, I suspect. Nigromancy! Since the Old Man's been sick, Thurtle's been running the home office, practically." Julian Thurtle was the head of the School of Shop Practice.

"So long, Clem," said Galt. "One of these days, the Dangerous Dane's gonna remember all those deposits you talked him outa, and take a poke at you."

"Grinnig's all right," grinned Buckminster. "He gets in fights because he's just an overgrown kid. That's it, an overgrown kid. But him and me get along fine. 'By." And Clem Buckminster, an inconspicuous figure of forty-odd with abundant but graying hair, went out softly singing:

> "Down with Harvard, down with Yale;
> We get our learning through the mail . . ."

Buckminster first sought Carl Grinnig at his normal place of employment, having assumed from Grinnig's wild talk that he was telephoning from there. But the shop head of the Alliance Oil Burner Co. informed Buckminster that the company's able but erratic mechanic was not in, allegedly because of sickness.

So the M. H. S. I. salesman rattled over to East Tremont Avenue and turned north toward the boardinghouse where Grinnig lived. This was a large, wooden, frame building with a front porch and wooden scrollwork.

At the first intersection, a policeman held up Buckminster's car with a decisive "Not this way, buddy!" Buckminster himself could see, beyond the cop, the backs of a small crowd of people, and over the heads of these the upperworks of a fire engine standing in front of Grinnig's house. He turned the car down a side street, parked, and walked toward the scene, observing that the house had several broken windows and that from these, dark streaks of smoke or char ran up the clapboarded sides of the house.

"Mr. Buckminster!" said a voice. It was that of Carl Grinnig, a large, powerful, blond young man with a black eye and a couple of purplish discolorations about the jaw. He seized a flabby Buckminster arm in one huge hand.

"Yeah?" said Buckminster, suppressing the desire to wince. "Had a fire?"

"Had a *fire?* Yust wait till I tell you—"

Grinnig's explanation was drowned by an outburst of sound: exclamations from the crowd, smothered curses from a couple of firemen who ran out of the house to the engine, from which they took a couple of chemical extinguishers and dashed back. People pointed toward a curl of smoke, which rose suddenly from one of the broken windows. Buckminster could hear people running about inside the house, and presently the smoke ceased.

A stout, harassed-looking civilian came out of the house and pushed through the people. Buckminster recognized the man as Grinnig's landlord. Grinnig called out: "Hey, Mr. Feldman! What is it this time?"

Feldman made motions of pulling nonexistent hair. "A book! A book up off the table I was lifting, just a ordinary book it was, and when I open it, into flames it bursts! Right in front of it the gentleman from the insurance company was standing. His own eyes he don't believe! Me, I'm going crazy!" The house owner departed distractedly.

"You see, Mr. Buckminster?" rumbled Grinnig. "It's been like this all morning. First it was a calendar on the wall went up, *whoof.* Then a mattress caught fire. This book's about the twentieth screwy fire. After the fire department had turned out for five or six of 'em, they yust left an engine here and guys sitting in every room with chemical extinguishers."

"Did you get hurt in the fires?" asked Buckminster, eying the mechanic's obvious contusions.

"Naw, that was just a little fight with a coupla sailors. Di'n't amount to nothing on account of there was only three of them. But I gotta see you, quick."

"What have I got to do with—" began the correspondence-course salesman, but Grinnig shushed him warningly.

"We gotta talk alone somewheres. Come on, maybe there ain't nobody in old man Feldman's garage." And Grinnig dragged Buckminster willy-nilly up the driveway, growled, "Beat it, you kids," to a pair of small boys who were watching events from the roof of the two-car garage, and shoved the salesman within.

"Look, Mr. Buckminster," said the mechanic, "it's that nigromancy course you sold me."

"What is?" queried Buckminster.

"That made these here fires. But don't you say nothing about it," he added ominously.

"Course I wouldn't," said Buckminster hastily. "After all, we got a reputation to protect, too. But how come the course had anything to do with the fires? Don't make sense. If you don't like it, why doncha change?"

"I'm not interested in changing my course, but in stopping these here fires!" persisted Grinnig.

"We got a swell new course in aviation mechanics," said Buckminster. "Wuncha like to be an aviation mechanic? Big future; not like messing around with these smelly oil boiners. You could make some real dough with—"

"Listen," said Grinnig with strained patience, "every time you sell me a new course, you tell me it'll make me rich. Well, I ain't rich. If they're so hot, why don't you take one? How come you're still selling 'em on commission and living on coffee and sinkers?"

Buckminster shook his head sadly. "Too late for me. Shoulda started when I was a young guy like you, steada playing around and wasting my dough. My future's behind me." (This was all fairly close to the truth.) "Now, about that avi—"

"Shut up!" bellowed Grinnig. "I don't wanna hear nothing about no new courses."

The burly mechanic fished out of a pocket a six-by-nine booklet with stiff, green paper covers. "Look at this thing!"

Buckminster read:

Mercury Home Study Institute
NIGROMANCY
by Julian A. Thurtle
(Dean, School of Shop Practice)
Volume 1   Conjuration of Saganes

He turned the cover and looked at the beginning of the text. It began:

1. *What nigromancy is.* The science of nigromancy was defined many years ago by Paracelsus (P. A. T. B. von Hohenheim) as the conjuration, control, and exorcism (banishment) of the elemental spirits of earth, air, fire, and water, called collectively Saganes. Since Paracelsus' time, the knowledge of this science has largely gone out of existence, so that today it is regarded by many as mere superstition. This is incorrect. Used with proper knowledge and care, this science can be as useful to modern technicians as any other. Accordingly, this course, based on recent research into some of the little-known writings of

Paracelsus and his contemporaries, has been prepared.

2. *Outline of the Course.* The first three volumes deal respectively with the conjuration, control, and banishment of elemental spirits. Students are warned not to attempt any experimental conjurations whatever until they have mastered at least three parts and have passed the examination at the end of each volume. The later volumes deal with the more advanced aspects of nigromancy and with allied subjects such as necromancy, hydromancy, enchantment, and sortilege—

Buckminster commented: "Now I know the home office is nuts. What happened?"

"Well," said Grinnig, "I wasn't feeling so good after I finished with those sailors, see? Musta been something I ate. So I called the shop and they said sure, I could have the day off. So I thought I'd see if this course would really do the things it said it would. So I look through the book and find a ritual for conjuring up a salamander. You know what a salamander is; one of those little red things like a lizard."

Buckminster put in: "It says here not to try no conjurations until you finish the first three lessons."

"Yeah, I know, but you think I'm gonna pay for a whole course if I don't know if it works? Anyway, I figure one of those little lizardy things couldn't do no damage."

"And it started the fires? G'wan!"

"Not the salamander; I mean, I didn't get no salamander, but a kind of a ball of fire. It ducked quick into a pair of work pants I had hanging up on my door and set 'em on fire. I grab the pants off the hook to beat the fire out, and the fireball dodges out through the crack of the door, so quick I can't hardly see it. And it's been flying around the house all morning setting fire to things."

"G'wan," repeated Buckminster. "Sure one of those sailors didn't clip you with a piece of pipe or somepin?"

"Naw," said Grinnig scornfully. "I seen what I seen. And I figure I gotta have the third volume of the course right now, on account of it tells how to get rid of these things."

"You can't," replied the salesman. "The second volume oughta be just about off the press, and the third ain't even printed. Anyway, I think you imagined it. Come down to the corner and I'll buy you a beer and tell you about how to be an aviation mechanic."

"I did not imagine it," persisted Grinnig.

"Okay, then, show me how you did it."

"Okay, wise guy, I'll show you. Gimme the book." Grinnig fished out the stub of a pencil, frowned over the diagrams, and slowly drew a number of complicated lines on the concrete floor of the garage. He took out a candle no longer than his thumb, lit it, and placed it on the floor. Then he mumbled a long series of sounds that sounded to Buckminster like continuous double-talk, pausing now and then to draw imaginary figures in the air with his pencil.

Carl Grinnig ended his spiel and shut the lesson book. "Aw right, Mr. Buckminster, you— Yumping Yudas!"

Over one of the diagrams, about ten feet from the two men, something was swiftly materializing. First came smoke and a smell of sulphur dioxide, then a dull-red glow, which brightened to orange. Then they were confronted by what looked like the nude iron statue of a powerfully built man at incandescent temperatures. The heat from the apparition beat on their faces like the glow from an open furnace door, and they began to sweat.

The fire man surveyed Buckminster and Grinnig. When he spoke, it was in a deep, harsh, strongly accented voice: "Where—is—my—liddle—creature?"

"I dunno what you're talking about," said Grinnig, his fair skin paler than usual.

"Please, mister, go away," added Buckminster. "It's all a mistake!"

"Ha," rasped the newcomer. "Mistake. Mistake. But few mistakes does your trade allow. Where is my salamander?"

Grinnig swallowed and croaked: "You mean that fire thing? It's in that big house in back of you."

The visitor turned his massive head and whistled piercingly. Almost immediately, a sphere of flickering orange flame the size of a soft baseball arrived with a rush, danced up and down in front of its master, and at length snuggled up under his armpit.

The glowing head raised slightly, and the men felt by the increase of heat rather than saw the glowing eyeballs fasten upon them. "And now," said the fire man, "wherefore have ye broken the Treaty?"

"What treaty?" said Grinnig.

"Ye know not? Ha." The apparition put out a hand to lean against the wooden side of the garage. There was an immediate burst of smoke where the hand touched the wall.

"Hi!" yelped Buckminster. The fire man took his hand away with a slight, grim smile, leaving a charred spot the shape of a hand on the wood.

"What, then, *do* ye know?" he demanded.

"N-not so much," quavered the massive Grinnig. "I yust got this little book from the Mercury Home Study Institute, and I wanted to try it out. So I did a little spell. Please, buddy, who are you and when are you going to let us out of here? It's damned hot!"

The thing smiled even more broadly. "Ye know not my real name even? Ye cannot control me?"

"I ain't come to that part of the course—"

"Ha! 'Tis rare fortune, indeed, that the Covenant should be breached by a brace of such witless bunglers as ye! This much will I tell you: that I am of the race of the

Saldines, which the meddling Paracelsus ignorantly called Rolamandri; one of the peoples of the fire world, even as my little salamander is one of the beasts of the world. When my pet vanished, I suspected some foul doings in your world and watched for another opening of the door, the same which you forthwith furnished me. Ha! Now truly shall Fire come into its own!"

"Whatcha mean?" piped Buckminster.

"I'll show you what I mean! Give me that book!"

Grinnig extended the lesson booklet, and snatched his hand back as the red-hot arm shot out to seize the volume, which instantly went up in a puff of flame.

"Freeze it!" roared the fire elemental. "I should have bethought me of the perishability of your paper. Where can I obtain another such volume?"

"I dunno," babbled Buckminster, "unless you wanna go clear out to Paterson."

"Where?"

"Paterson, New Jersey, where the home office is. They got the whole course out there."

"Then let us forth. But stay! I cannot move abroad without some garment, lest I attract the attention of the general."

"I'll say you would," murmured Buckminster. "You'd attract the whole army."

"Give me, then, your clothing."

"Hey!" squawked the salesman. "They're too small for you, and anyway they'd burn up if you tried to put 'em on!"

"True," growled the Saldine. "I have it! There exists in your world a substance known before the Treaty as salamander skin, which in sooth is but a fabric woven of the strands of a certain fibrous rock. Fetch me a suit of this forthwith!"

"He means asbestos," explained Grinnig.

"Yeah, but how—"

"Fetch it!" thundered the Saldine, "ere I set my pet upon you!" He plucked the salamander from under his armpit and whispered to it. It zipped over close to the men and bobbed menacingly about them. They could feel its heat even in that oven atmosphere.

The elemental added: "But one of you; the smaller. The other shall remain as hostage, and do ye but essay any treason or alarums, I'll embrace the fellow *thus!*" He grinned fiendishly and wrung an imaginary dishrag with his huge, fiery hands.

"Okay," capitulated Buckminster. "Got any dough, Carl?"

Grinnig wordlessly handed over his wallet. The elemental stood aside long enough to let Buckminster, wincing at the scorching radiation, duck out the garage door. The Saldine called the salamander back to him and fell into a statuesque pose in the doorway, arms folded across his mighty chest and feet spread.

Carl Grinnig, seeing the only easy exit blocked again, sat down wearily on the concrete floor. In the ensuing wait, he recovered some of his aplomb. Although he did not feel like a particularly dangerous Dane, he was too big and tough to be completely intimidated for long.

He remarked: "You never told me who you really are and what you want."

"Ha!" barked the Saldine and relapsed into silence.

"Okay, then I'll have to call you Arson."

"Arson?" The being grinned. "A good name, forsooth. How good, ye have yet no notion."

"How come you talk so funny?"

"Talk so funny?" frowned Arson. "What mean ye? Verily, I speak what was the best English at the time of the Treaty, in your year 1623. I can comprehend that the tongue may have degenerated since then."

Grinnig shed his dripping shirt. A package of cigarettes

flopped out of the breast pocket; he took one out and lit it, and blew out the match.

"You!" shouted the elemental suddenly, and advanced with menacing steps. "What mean ye by destroying Fire, in my very presence?"

"B-but . . . I just blew out the match. You wouldn't want me to burn my fingers? Or would you?" Grinnig flattened himself against the rear wall of the garage as the heat became intolerable.

"For that," thundered Arson, "ye shall— But not yet, for I need you as hostage. 'Tis such vile comportment that marks you and your kind for their just deserts! I am even informed that ye keep whole companies of men trained to quench fires!"

"You mean the fire departments?" sweated Grinnig. "Yeah, when a house catches fire, they try to put it out, natchly."

"Foul, wanton vandalism!" cried the Saldine. "When my brethren come—" He closed his mouth with a snap and retired, leaving Grinnig red of skin and half fainting from the roasting he had received.

"Hey, Mr. Grinnig!" called Clem Buckminster from outside the garage. "Tell him I got his stuff!"

Arson stood aside to admit the salesman with an armful of canvaslike material.

Buckminster explained: "I got it from a fire-apparatus company; it's one of these here asbestos suits. Got shoes and gloves. I borrowed a pair of tinsnips and some wire and fixed the helmet up so it looks almost like a hat. Looky. Took all our dough, even though it's secondhand."

While Buckminster chuckled with naïve pleasure over his ingenuity, the elemental pulled on the suit. When it was all in place and he had put on the altered helmet, he looked quite human except for the orange glow of the face that glared out from under the hat brim. Otherwise he might have been an ash collector or some other dirty-job worker in the costume of his calling. The two men drew long breaths of relief as the searing heat rays were cut off for the nonce.

"Come!" commanded Arson. "To Paterson, Oo Jersey!" He cuffed them roughly ahead of him out of the garage and down the driveway, pausing to cast a speculative eye at Feldman's boardinghouse.

The fire engine was gone from the curb, although a couple of firemen were still in evidence. Several people were stacking furniture in the back yard. None paid attention to the trio, for in the bright sunlight, even the incandescence of Arson's face was not noticeable unless one looked closely.

The Saldine muttered: "Right well has my little pet done, and he shall yet have an opportunity to finish his task. Would I could stop to attend the matter myself! Go on, ye two!"

"Hey!" wailed Buckminster. "Are we gonna walk the whole way?"

"Of a certainty, unless you can provide a conveyance."

The salesman glanced down the street to where his car was parked, its stern just visible around the corner. "I got my car, but—"

"But what?"

"There wouldn't be room for all three of us, and anyway you'd burn it up!"

"Ha," said Arson flatly. He looked about. In the opposite direction a coal truck stood at the curb a block away. He pointed. "Is that one of your conveyances?"

"Yeah, it runs, if that's whatcha mean."

"Then shall we take it. It looks to be made of fire-resisting material."

"But it ain't ours! You can't just steal a truck like that!"

"Say you so?" snarled the fire man. He moved his arms,

and the salamander appeared, bobbing up and down from the palm of his outstretched hand. "Shall I set my pet—"

"No, no," amended Buckminster quickly.

As they approached the truck, the men's hearts sank as they observed it to be unoccupied.

"The large one," announced Arson, "shall mount the rear of the conveyance with me. The other shall drive."

Grinnig hesitated just long enough for the elemental to make a move as if to seize him and throw him up into the empty truck bodily; the mechanic scrambled quickly up under his own power. Arson followed more deliberately. The truck's springs creaked as though a considerable load had been added.

When Buckminster nervously slid into the driver's seat, the Saldine banged on the back of the cab. "Can ye hear me?" he bellowed.

"Yeah, sure."

"Good. To Paterson, Oo Jersey, and swiftly!"

To get accustomed to the ponderous vehicle took Clem Buckminster several miles, and then he came to one of the approaches of the George Washington Bridge. Just before he reached the approach, it occurred to him that perhaps trucks were not allowed on the bridge. While he slowed the truck, torn between fear of Arson and fear of the law, a second thought told him that to get pinched was exactly what he wanted. On his whole trip from East Tremont Avenue, he had not seen a single policeman, who belong to a species that vanish like the snows in spring whenever one had a real need for them.

An occasional smell whiffed through the driver's cab; undoubtedly, thought Buckminster, scorched paint. The asbestos suit would eventually warm up so that it radiated almost as much heat as the naked Arson. He pushed the accelerator to the floor as the truck crested the middle of the bridge roadway and roared down the long slope toward the toll booths on the Jersey side.

He began to slow down as the distant blue-coated figures of the toll collectors came into view. Then a banging on the back of the cab informed him that Arson had words for him. They were: "Hasten! No stopping!" When Buckminster continued to apply the brake, he heard a shriek from Grinnig. Arson had snatched off a glove and thrust a fiery hand close to the luckless mechanic's face.

Clem Buckminster speeded up again, looking for a toll booth before which no autos were lined up. He found one, to his disappointment. Well, maybe the truck was too big to squeeze through the restricted opening and would get stuck between the concrete piers. If he had had suicidal courage, he might have chanced deliberately ramming an obstacle, but he was not that kind of person. He sighted on the opening as best he could and steered right through without even scratching the paint.

He was in the midst of the tangle of ramps west of the bridge when he at long last heard the welcome *we-e-e-e-ew* of a siren. Now he *had* to stop. As he slowed, a motorcycle pulled alongside. The cop pointed: "Down there!"

Buckminster steered into the less-used ramp indicated and came out on an ordinary street, where he stopped. The cop parked his cycle ahead of the truck and walked back. As he took out his pad he looked up at the cab with an expression more of pity than of anger. He said:

"Say, buddy, don't you know *anything* about the traffic laws?"

When Buckminster could not answer, the policeman added: "A grown man like you oughta know you can't drive ya truck across the bridge at fifty—"

"Ain't my truck," croaked Buckminster.

"Now listen, buddy, it don't matter whether you're hired to drive—"

"I stole it, see?" said the salesman.

At this the policeman's voice simply dried up, and he stared with his mouth open until a motion on the curb side of the truck attracted his attention. This was Arson, who had descended from the truck body and was walking forward to the motorcycle. The elemental bent over the vehicle with interest.

"Hey, leggo that!" yelled the cop as Arson experimentally wiggled the handle bars.

The Saldine ignored the command and removed his gloves for more intimate contact. As the policeman started toward him, he clamped his red-hot hands on the framework, picked the cycle up, and with a creaking of tortured metal calmly twisted the whole thing out of shape.

Buckminster could see the paint beginning to curl and smoke. A tire burst into flame. Then, with a loud *whoof,* the gasoline tank went off, and Arson was completely hidden in a vast cloud of flame and smoke. The cop jumped back and banged his elbow against a fender of the truck.

When the smoke cleared and the flames subsided, Arson was standing in a small sea of burning gasoline and still holding the blazing wreck of the cycle. He was unchanged except that his asbestos suit was of a dirtier gray than before.

"It ain't . . . isn't real," said the cop to himself, rubbing his elbow.

The elemental now started toward the policeman, an evil grin on his glowing face. As he tramped he raised the motorcycle over his head. The cop shouted something which Buckminster missed, then drew his pistol. The gun barked three times, at a range where a miss was impossible. Each shot was followed by a metallic clang such as one hears after a hit on a shooting-gallery target. Arson grinned more widely and hurled the motorcycle. The cop ducked, but a handle bar struck his head and he tumbled to the concrete as the cycle whizzed past the cab window.

Arson in leisurely manner walked back and climbed into the truck. Far down the street a few civilians were standing and watching, but none seemed eager to investigate. "Hence!" roared the Saldine through the back of the cab.

As he started the truck again, Clem Buckminster, for the first time in some years, prayed.

Before the truck came to the bridge over the Passaic River, the heat and stench which Buckminster now automatically associated with the presence of Arson became too strong for comfort even inside the cab. A glance in the mirror showed a fair-sized cloud of smoke billowing out from the truck body. As the salesman began to slow the vehicle again, there was a muffled explosion and a burst of flame. The temperature soared alarmingly.

Buckminster pulled on the hand brake and swerved the truck off the road into the weeds. He scrambled out before it stopped rolling, to find the rear half of the truck enveloped in flames and Grinnig and the elemental already descended to earth. The mechanic was a pitiful sight, with blistered hands and singed eyebrows, and black with sweat-streaked coal dust.

"How much farther?" growled the Saldine.

"Coupla miles," said Buckminster resignedly.

"Good. We shall walk!" And Arson, shooing the men ahead of him, set out at a brisk stride.

When they had gone a few hundred yards from the conflagration, a car stopped to investigate the burning truck, and another, until there was a traffic jam on that section of the road. A police siren whined.

"Continue to wend," snapped Arson, "and look not back!"

They passed a section of road that was being widened, although no workmen were in sight at the moment. Several pieces of road machinery stood around on the new strip with canvas covers over their works.

"Conveyances!" muttered Arson. "Let us take another for our own use, as the journey grows tedious."

"Hey!" bleated Buckminster. "The gas tanks'll blow up if you get aboard, same as the truck did!"

"That," grinned the elemental nastily, "will be your misfortune!" He inspected a bulldozer. "Into the driver's seat, small one!"

"Won't do no good, Mr. Arson," protested Buckminster. "Gas tank's empty. See this here gauge?"

"Another, then," snorted Arson. But all the other pieces of equipment proved to have empty fuel tanks as well, the contractor having thriftily drained them before temporarily laying them up.

The last two machines inspected were a pair of road rollers; one a modern gasoline roller, the other an old-fashioned steam roller with a vertical boiler. This, too, lacked fuel, but investigation disclosed that it had water in its boiler.

Arson remarked: "I begin to fathom the operation of these devices. Yet this one appeareth to be of a nature different from the others. What is the quintessence of its active principle?"

Grinnig huskily explained the essentials of steam-engine operation.

"Ha!" grinned Arson. "Whereas it needs nought but a modicum of heat for its operation, forsooth I will furnish that!" He opened the door of the fire box, climbed onto the body, removed a shoe, and thrust a glowing foot into the opening. After a few minutes' wait, the elemental exclaimed: "Why starts this conveyance not? I wax impatient! O fool, think ye to deceive me?"

"No, no!" chirped Buckminster. "Look at the gauge; she'll have steam pressure up any time now!"

They fell into silence, waiting, Buckminster hoping

that by some miracle the United States Army would descend on them to rescue him and his student and subdue Mr. Arson, if need be with heavy artillery. But nothing of the sort occurred; automobiles purred by indifferently. Buckminster was bright enough to guess that to yell "Help!" to one or two uncomprehending and ineffective civilians would merely make a bad situation worse.

At last steam was up. Buckminster opened the throttle and spun the steering wheel, which was connected to the forward roller by a worm gear and a chain. With a rapid *pop-pop-pop*, the machine shudderingly ground over the unfinished road surface, and on the highway, and rattled on into Paterson.

Buckminster stopped the roller and pointed to a group of slightly dilapidated buildings that occupied one of Paterson's outlying blocks. "That's them," he explained. "The Mercury Home Study Institute."

As the party approached the nearest building, Buckminster thought furiously. Arson's vague threats had certainly implied that the fire elemental was up to no good. The salesman suspected that the Saldine wanted to get control of a set of the course booklets in order to conjure up more of his fiendish kind. But if he, Clem, could get hold of one of those booklets first, notably the ones dealing with the control and banishment of elementals, perhaps he could beat Arson to the punch.

So it was in a state of extreme alertness that Buckminster approached the building housing the Mercury printing establishment. He turned to Arson and said:

"The books are all in there. You wait here and I'll—"

"Ha, think you I'm such a dunce? Lead on and I'll follow!"

"But you'll set this old building on fire—"

A shove sent Buckminster staggering toward the nearest doorway. He shrugged and went in, Grinnig and

Arson following. The elemental left black footprints of charred wood on the aged floor.

Down one side of the printshop ran a row of a dozen flat-bed presses, about half of which were in action, their beds weaving back and forth under the cylinders with a continuous loud grumble. On the other side of the aisle along the presses was a row of low hand trucks, each of which bore a pile of large white sheets, varying from a foot to four feet in height. Some of these piles were fresh paper for the presses, some had been printed on one side only and some had been printed on both sides and were waiting to be fed to the folding machines in the bindery, which occupied the other half of the building. At the far end of the bindery were a lot of hand trucks of another kind, on which were stacked hundreds of completed green Mercury lesson booklets and sets of advertising literature. The first printing of Volume 1 of the nigromancy course would probably be here, unless it had been taken over to the school building, whence the booklets were mailed to students and where the students' examinations were corrected.

Buckminster moved slowly down the line of trucks bearing the stacks of big squares of paper. He suppressed a whoop as he found what he wanted: a pile of printed sheets, each sheet having forty-eight pages of text on each side, and among the pages the first page of a Mercury booklet, with a heading:

NIGROMANCY
Volume 2   Control of Saganes

Buckminster ran his eye hastily over the sheet but encountered a difficulty. The pages were not grouped on the sheet in the order in which they would be read, but were so arranged that when the sheet was put in the folding machine, and folded and cut and folded and cut down to final form, these pages would then be in the proper order.

Nevertheless, Buckminster ran over the pages quickly, regardless of the fact that half of them were on the underside of the sheet and half the remainder were upside down. Sure enough, a subtitle caught his eye:

12. *Control of Trifertes (Fire Elementals).* The salamander, being a trifertis of relatively low intelligence, is comparatively easy to control—

"Excuse me," said a voice behind him, "but have you gents got permission from the office to look around the shop?"

Buckminster started guiltily; then recognized the foreman of the printshop. He said:

"Hello, Jim; 'member me? Clem Buckminster, from the New York office."

"Hello," said the foreman mechanically. "It's pret' near quitting time, you know, and you'll have to—"

"Can you lend me a pencil, Jim?" asked Buckminster quickly. The foreman handed one over, and Buckminster, referring back to the printed sheet, began to draw figures on the floor.

"Ho!" muttered Arson suddenly. "What do ye, wretch?"

The foreman looked at the elemental closely for the first time and backed away in alarm as he observed the orange glow of the Saldine's visage, which was fairly conspicuous indoors.

"Hey," he said, "who is this?"

"Mr. Arson, meet Mr. Slezak," mumbled Buckminster.

"But—what's the matter with him?"

"He got sunburned, out at Jones Beach," explained the salesman, frowning as he realized that he would have to turn the print sheet over to get the information necessary to complete his ritual.

"I'll say he got burned," said Slezak. "You gotta use discretion. I got some good suntan oil that—"

"I see!" roared Arson. "Ye prepare a spell for me, eh? Bah!" The elemental snatched off his gloves, stuck them between his teeth, and began to assault the pile of sheets with his glowing hands. The upper sheets at once began to burn. Arson whipped them off in great handfuls, crumpled them, and tosssed them, flaming, right and left.

Cries of alarm rang through the printery as smoke and pieces of burning paper rose and spread. At that moment, the five-o'clock bell rang. The printers shut down their presses and raced for the doors, Buckminster and Grinnig among them. The whole middle of the printery was now a mass of blazing paper, from whose invisible center Arson roared with demoniac laughter.

Buckminster caught Grinnig's belt in the rear and hung on lest they be separated in the rush. When they had put a respectable distance between themselves and the now furiously smoking building, they looked back. Workmen were scattered all over the intervening area; clerks and instructors poured out of the school building. Among these Buckminster recognized a small group of men in coats and neckties as the executives.

"Come on," he said to Grinnig. "If we can find Thurtle, maybe we can fix Arson's wagon."

A policeman cleared a way for the fire engines. Buckminster and Grinnig worked their way around the cleared area to where the executives stood. The former called:

"Oh, Mr. Thurtle!"

Julian Thurtle, dean of the School of Shop Practice of the Mercury Home Study Institute, looked about as much like a chimpanzee with a white handle-bar mustache as a man can without actually being a chimpanzee with a white handle-bar mustache. But he was a wise old teacher of technics whose courses, the texts for many of which he wrote himself, were up to college standards and had actually helped many ambitious young men on their way to success, as claimed in his company's advertisements.

He was conversing with the vice president in charge of sales, who was saying: "—of course, it's all insured, but it'll raise Ned with our publishing schedule, not to mention interrupting a lot of the courses. The Education Everywhere Institute won't be sorry to hear of it."

Thurtle sighed. "Yes, yes. Dear me. Maybe we could persuade the I. C. C. to help us out; they're pretty decent fellows—" He saw Buckminster and said: "Yes? Yes? You are . . . don't tell me . . . Buckmaster of the Philadelphia office, aren't you?"

The salesman corrected him and asked: "Can I see you a minute—"

"Not now, not now, my dear fellow. This is too important. Go on, get your hoses inside the building, you. . . . you twerps!" The last sentence was addressed in a low voice to the distant firemen.

A policeman approached with a pad in hand. He said: "Oh, Mr. Thurtle—"

"Yes? Yes? Oh, hello, Bill. What—"

"There was an alarm sent out for a gang of pyromaniacs that's terrorizing northern New Jersey," said the cop. "They burned a truck and a coupla houses, and they knocked a cop unconscious at the George Washington Bridge. I was wondering if they mightn't have something to do with this—"

"Yes. No. Dear me, I don't know. I'm too upset, officer."

"Okay, Mr. Thurtle," said the cop and wandered off.

Then there were sudden cries from the crowd. A crew of firemen were advancing on a doorway with a hose, which they played through the aperture, when a large figure in shapeless gray garments came out that door from the burning building. The stream of water from the hose struck the figure squarely, but instead of knocking him back into the building as it should have done, it gave a colossal hiss and turned into a vast cloud of steam. Some witnesses, including Clem Buckminster, had a glimpse of the gray figure dodging out of the steam cloud and vanishing around the corner of the building.

"Good gracious," said Thurtle. "What—"

Buckminster cried: "That's what I wanna see you about, Mr. Thurtle! This here is Carl Grinnig, who got the first lesson in that new course of yours!"

"Oh." Comprehension dawned in Thurtle's eyes, and he followed the salesman unprotesting.

When they were out of earshot of the spectators, Buckminster gave a brief account of events.

"This is terrible!" exclaimed Thurtle. "Mr. Grinnig, you should never have tried an incantation before—"

"How was *I* to know—" protested Grinnig.

"You couldn't; it was partly my fault, too. I should never have put out that course. The only reason I did it was that I hated to see all that powerful scientific knowledge going to waste, and I did want to put one over on our competitors. I got hold of a copy of Paracelsus' *'Ex Libris de Nymphis, Sylvanis, etc.';* not the abridgment published by Nissensis of Danzic in 1566, which omits all the effective spells, but the last original— Well, that's water over the dam; the question is, what'll we do?"

"I was just gonna ask you that," said Buckminster.

"Yes, yes, I suppose so. It's a difficult problem. From what you've told me, the Rolamander is practically indestructible by physical means; water and bullets don't bother him in the least."

"How about freezing him?" asked Grinnig.

"I don't know; I think you'd practically have to incase him in an iceberg. He gets his energy from the fire world."

Buckminster here suggested: "Maybe we could lure him into a big refrigerator and shut the door!"

"Not likely; he's too crafty."

"We could call out the army," said Grinnig hopefully. "They could bomb him."

"Perhaps; but the time we convinced them, he'd have found a way to let his fellow hellions into this world."

Buckminster asked: "What does he wanna do that for?"

"To burn everything combustible, I suspect. And don't ask me why they want to burn things. They just do."

"Unreasonable sorta guys," commented the little salesman.

"Not necessarily; it's that their scale of moral values is entirely different from ours. We can't understand them. Fire's a good servant but an ill master, you know. Let's see; let's see. The printed nigromancy course is no more; the first two volumes were all in the printshop, except for Grinnig's copy, and those that weren't burned up will be ruined by the water. The manuscript in the typesetting room went, too, I fancy. There remains only my copy of the manuscript. Neither we nor Mr. Arson want that destroyed; we want to use it to banish him, and he wants to use it to invoke his fellow Rolamanders. But if he finds us with it, he'll force us to perform the conjuration spell on pain of a horrible death, since he can't handle the papers himself without burning them."

Buckminster asked: "Couldn't we pretend to do the conjuring spell, but really do the banishing spell?"

"That's the trouble; he'd know in a minute we were trying to fool him, and with his fiery disposition you can imagine what would happen. These spells aren't simple things that you can say 'hocus pocus' and the elemental vanishes, you know. Since he escaped from Grinnig's control, we'd have to get him back into a servile state first, and I confess I'm not sure how to do it. Dear, dear. Oh, what's he wearing?"

"An asbestos fire fighter's suit," responded Buckminster.

"Aha, now perhaps—" Thurtle broke off and stared past the other two men, horror growing in his face.

"Ha!" The rasping monosyllable and the feeling of warmth on their backs told Buckminster and Grinnig that their enemy was behind them. "Foolish wights, I grow weary of these pastimes. Fetch me forthwith a set of the rest of those books!"

Thurtle spoke: "I . . . I'm sorry, Mr. Arson, but they're all destroyed. No, no, don't blame us, old fellow; you started the fire yourself!"

"So I did," grinned Arson. "But I know something of the habits of you of the Cold World. Do not try to tell me that all copies of the work were burned up; you would have an extra somewhere. Lead me to it, and attempt no stratagems such as burning it, unless you wish a speedy but painful death."

"I swear there are no more copies!" cried Thurtle. But Arson simply grinned more widely and began to toss his salamander meaningfully from hand to hand.

"Will you lead me to it, for the last time?" purred the elemental.

"I tell you it doesn't ex—" That was as far as Julian Thurtle got, for the salamander swooped at him and ignited one end of his magnificent mustache. Thurtle, with a small shriek, clapped a hand to smother the blaze. When he removed the hand, the right side of the mustace was intact, but of the left wing only a short black stubble on the upper lip remained. The salamander whirled in a small circle around the dean's head.

"All right," groaned Thurtle. "Follow me."

He led them for several blocks into a grimy district, whose buildings were largely devoted to the sale of raw materials, chemicals, and agricultural and industrial machinery. There were few people on the depressing street, most of the people who did business in this neighborhood having gone home to supper.

"Hasten," growled Arson, "for it grows dark, and I cannot wander abroad in this village at night with my face lighting the way like a beacon." His face was in fact becoming pretty conspicuous, though the sun would not set for another hour.

Thurtle stopped the procession in front of an old wooden frame building bearing the sign:

WILLIAMS & GIBBON
Welding Equipment & Supplies

Buckminster almost asked why the devil Thurtle chose to keep the spare copy of his manuscript in such a place, but thought better of it. Thurtle himself said: "Wait here, Mr. Arson, and I'll get the papers."

"Ha, so think you. I'll come with you—"

"Oh, no, you won't, unless you want to set this house on fire, too! Then there really wouldn't be any more copies."

"Very well," grumbled the fire elemental. "I will keep these two as hostages. Do you but attempt a spell behind my back, I shall know, and do them most horribly die!"

Thurtle darted into the building, called, "Tom!" and ran up the stairs.

Buckminster and Grinnig remained uneasily with Arson, who had taken up his statuesque pose in front of the doorway. Buckminster was badly frightened; he was sure that Thurtle was up to something, that it might not work, and that Arson would take it out on him and Grinnig. Maybe the old boy would destroy the manuscript, which would prevent further invocations of elementals, but would leave the invulnerable and vindictive Arson abroad in this world. Buckminster clenched his jaw to keep his teeth from chattering.

A window creaked overhead. Carl Grinnig was too far gone to look up. Clem Buckminster would ordinarily have done so had not the crisis given his otherwise mediocre wits a preternatural sharpness. He fought to control his eyes and face, lest he betray his knowledge of things taking place on the second-story level.

There was a brilliant white flare of light.

Several persons claimed afterward to have seen what happened, but they saw from a distance of a block or more, did not begin to notice until the process was well under way, and told stories differing so widely from each other and from the version of Julian Thurtle, an eminent and respected citizen, that not much credence was given these stories.

The flare was caused by the lighting of a magnesium ribbon stuck in the top of a bucket of gray powder, which Thurtle and his acquaintance, Tom Gibbon, had lowered on a wire from the upstairs window until it was a foot or so over Arson's unsuspecting head. Right after the flash the bottom of the bucket fell out, and a cascade of blindingly incandescent material poured down over Arson while the elemental was just beginning to look up to see what was going on.

Buckminster and Grinnig staggered back, shielding their faces from the scorching heat and blinding light. Buckminster blinked for a few seconds before he could see anything at all.

Where Arson had stood was a shapeless thing about half the stature of a man, which sank and slumped and ran out, across the sidewalk, up and down the gutter, spreading scintillating whiteness over an area twenty feet across. The glare dimmed to a mere yellow that could be looked at directly without scorching the eyeballs, and Julian Thurtle from the upstairs window called: "Fire! You, Buckmaster, turn in the alarm!" In truth, the front of Williams & Gibbon's building had begun to burn; little flames ran up the door posts in businesslike fashion.

An alarm had already been turned in. In a few minutes, a fire truck extended a ladder up to the window. Thurtle and Gibbon scrambled down it, slightly smoke-blackened but otherwise unhurt.

"No, no, no, thank you," Thurtle said to those who helped him off the ladder and asked if he wanted hospitalization. "I'm not hurt, really. Perhaps this poor boy, who tried to get up the stairs to us—" He indicated Grinnig, who displayed several minor burns from his previous experiences.

"Naw," said Grinnig. He grinned and tugged Thurtle and Buckminster aside. "Hey, doc," he said to the former, "whad ya do to the guy?"

"I melted him," said Thurtle.

"What with?"

"Thermite! Arson thought he was pretty hot, but you bet he wasn't so hot as that thermite! I knew Williams & Gibbon had some thermite on their place, and I got Tom Gibbon to help me with the bucket and the fuse.

"That's all, except that if you fellows take my advice, you won't try to tell anyone about Arson or the nigromancy course—which is all gone now anyway—or your adventures today. I'm going to forget the course and stick that manuscript away in a sort of private time capsule."

"I getcha, boss," said Buckminster. "Say, Carl, hadn't we better stop in at a drugstore and smear some of that tannic-acid junk on ya burns?"

Grinnig looked at his blackened hands. "The main thing I want is yust to get washed up."

"Okay, this here joint oughta have a washroom. And while we're fixing you up, I'll tell you all about our swell

new course on how to be an aviation mechanic. We'll
have to switch you to a new one, and you wanna make
some real dough, doncha? Okay. Hey, wassamatta, Carl?
I didn't say nothing! HELP!"

   Sock!

KA THE APPALLING

As he ran through the streets of Typhon, Gezun of Gadaira recalled the words of the Ausonian adept he had met in Maxia:

"Typhon rises in black and purple from the mystic margins of the Sea of Thesh, amid the towering tombs of kings who reigned in splendor over Setesh when mighty Torrutseish was but a village and golden Kernê but an empty stretch of beach. No man knows the total tale of Typhon's history, or the convolutions of its streets and secret passages, or the hoarded treasure of its kings, or the hidden powers of its wizards . . ."

Just now, Gezun would gladly have given the hoarded treasure of the Seteshan kings to be carried far from this accursed place. For a youth of nineteen, he had seen much since slavers had stolen him from his home in windy Lorsk in Pusâd, or Poseidonis as the Hesperians called it. But he had never seen a city where people tried to tear a man to bits for killing a cat.

He rounded a corner as stones whizzed past him. If there had been only a few Typhonians, he would not have fled. As it was, he had laid out two with his staff before the throng had become too many to handle, even though he was nearly twice their size.

For the Seteshans were a small people, dark, slender, hatchet-faced, and scant of beard, while Gezun was a typical Lorska: over six feet before he had reached his full growth, with the bold, rugged features, the big, sharp nose, beetling brow, and square, jutting jaw of his folk. His skin was almost as dark as a Seteshan's. His hair was thick, black, and curly, and he had a respectable beard despite his youth. A girl in Yavan had told him he looked like a god—not the grim sort of god who broods on people's sins and dispenses doom by thunderbolts, but the kind who roams the earth teaching people to make wine and looking for likely mortal maids on whom to get demigods.

In the open, he could have outrun most Seteshans. But in these twisted streets, he hesitated at turnings long enough to let the mob gain back what they had lost in the straight stretches. Furthermore, with such a large crowd, there were bound to be some swift runners. These pressed to the front. Their teeth gleamed, their eyes glared, and foam blew back from their chins. They bore knives, stones, bricks—whatever they had snatched up. Their panting breaths were like the hissing of a thousand snakes.

Gezun passed a tavern where a pair of King Zeremab's archers lounged in the doorway. He slid to a stop and pointed back at the mob.

"They—look—help me—" he gasped.

The soldiers glanced. The mob shrieked: "Slay the cat-killer! Burn the blasphemer! Flay the foul foreigner!"

The soldiers looked at one another. One cried: "Slay the foreign devil!" and drew his dagger.

Gezun hit him over the ear with his staff and knocked him sprawling. The other archer started forward but fell over his companion. Gezun ran on, a corner of his cloak flapping behind him like a flag.

Passing a potter's stall, he jerked the rack of finished pots so that it fell forward with a crash, filling the street with bouncing, rolling, and smashing pots. The obstacle hardly checked the mob. The leaders cleared the pots in long leaps. The rest flowed over them like some natural force. A few fell, but the rest trampled on and scrambled over the fallen, heedless of what bones of their own folk they broke if they could only get at the hated alien.

Another corner. Gezun's teeth showed, too, as he gasped. His staff got heavier with every stride. Should he throw it away or keep it for his last stand? He had a short, bronze, Tartessian sword under his cloak, but with the staff he might be able to hold the mob at arms' length. The sword, although deadlier, would let them close enough to fasten on him like the giant leeches of the Tritonian Sea and pull him down.

With a burst of speed, Gezun gained enough so that he turned one corner before the mob rounded the last one. Coming out upon a street in which Gezun was not to be seen, the mob hesitated before dividing like a stream of ants, half going each way.

Gezun made another turn, into a mere alley, not wide enough to let two men pass unless they sidled past one another. It was so crooked that he could see along it only a few paces. On either side rose high walls of stone or brick, without openings save, once in a while, a stout wooden door. Gezun knew enough of Seteshan customs not to expect help there.

The alley ended. Gezun faced another wall across his path. He was in a cul-de-sac. The walls rose smoothly around him, except where to one side was a gap a pace wide between two houses. The space was blocked up to the height of a man by a mass of rubble from some earlier edifice, which had been simply pushed into the place between the houses when they were built. A man could climb over the fallen masonry, but beyond it rose the wall of still another house. So the space between the houses formed a minor cul-de-sac, branching off from the main one.

The sound of the mob, muted for the moment, rose again. Plainly, they were coming down the alley to see if he had taken refuge there. The crowd had put off an off-shoot, like a tendril, to probe all nearby cavities for its prey. In such a narrow space they could come at him only one or two at a time. If they were mere soldiers he might hold them off, at least until he dropped from exhaustion or somebody fetched a bow to shoot him.

But with a mob of fanatics, those behind would push those in front, willing or not, up against Gezun faster than he could knock or cut them down. So the end would be the same, with the swarm fastening on him, using teeth and nails if there was no room to wield a weapon. Teeth and nails would kill one just as dead as swords and spears, and rather more painfully.

Gezun pounded on the nearest door. The copper shutter that closed the peephole on the inside moved aside. A black Seteshan eye looked out.

"Let me in!" said Gezun. "I am beset!"

The shutter moved back into place. Gezun angrily thrust at it with his staff, but it held. He was not surprised. The noise of the mob grew louder.

The pile of rubble might make a better place for a last stand than the alley proper. Not only was the gap between the houses narrower, but also by mounting the pile one could make the pursuers climb up and whack them on the sconce as they came.

Gezun sprang into the gap and had begun to climb the pile when a voice said: "In here, foreign devil!"

Between the pile of rubble and the wall of the right-hand house, an opening had appeared. A face, obscured by the deep shadow, looked up.

"Hasten!" said the face.

The crowd noises sounded as if they were just around the next bend.

Gezun lowered his large feet into the hole and squeezed through. His feet found a dirt floor.

"Out of the way, fool!" said the face. The owner of the face pushed Gezun aside and thrust a piece of old, rotten wood into the opening. It cut off most of the light, although since the fit was not tight, some light came into the tunnel around the wood. The tunnel itself was not utterly dark. A flickering light came around the first bend.

"Come," said the man. He was a small, brown Seteshan in a long, dirty robe. He had sharp, irregular features and crooked teeth. He was bald save for gray tufts that stood out over each ear.

The man led the way down the tunnel, muttering: "Hurry, barbarian clod! They may poke around and find my tunnel. And watch your head."

The last advice was too late; Gezun had just hit his forehead on a crossbeam. The tunnel had been built for Seteshans, not towering Pusadians. The roof had been shored up by odd bits of timber, so that to walk through the tunnel one had to duck and dodge with every step.

Gezun followed, bent over, his head ringing. He still gasped from his run; his tunic was sweat-soaked.

Around the corner, a Seteshan girl held a rushlight. She walked ahead of the two men, shielding the light with her hand. The tunnel bent this way and that but seemed to be going deeper. The soil, powder-dry near the surface, became moist as they went down. The blistering heat of the Seteshan summer gave way to delicious cool.

The tunnel branched and forked. Gezun tried to remember his turnings but soon gave up.

The tunnel became a regular structure of dressed stone,

as if they had reached the crypt of some large building. They halted where the tunnel opened out into a series of rooms. The girl lit two more rushlights. Gezun saw that she was handsome in a slender, birdlike way, although she looked a little like the man. Like him, she had blue-black hair and an olive-brown skin.

"Sit," said the man.

Gezun sank down on a bench and threw off his cloak. He sat holding his head and drinking in the cool air. He sneezed, wiped the drying sweat from his face with a corner of his cloak, and said:

"How came you to save me?"

"I saw the start of the chase," said the man. "I went into my tunnels and later heard the sounds of the mob near another of my entrances. You must have circled round and nearly returned to your starting place."

"I don't know Typhon well."

"So I see. Who are you?"

"Gezun of Gadaira."

"Where is that?"

"Far to the west. I was born in Poseidonis."

"Of that I have heard; a sinking land in the sea."

"Who are you, sir?"

"Ugaph the son of Shepsaa. This is my daughter Ro. What do you so far from home?"

"I like to wander. I make a living as a wizard."

"*You* a wizard? Ha!"

"I was a pupil of the great Sancheth Sar."

"I never heard of him, and if he was not a Seteshan he cannot have amounted to much."

Gezun shrugged. "I let my clients praise me."

"When got you here?"

"Yesterday. I was strolling about, minding my own business—"

"Slowly, or I cannot understand. You speak our tongue barbarously."

"I was minding my own business and enjoying the sights of the city when your people tried to kill me."

"What led you to do so mad a thing as to slay a cat?"

"I bought a loaf and a fish in the agora for my dinner. Then I went to a tavern by the side of the agora. I bought a mug of barley beer, and the taverner cooked my fish. I had my dinner laid out on the table outside the tavern and had just turned my head to look at a pretty girl, when this wretched cat leaped to the table and made off with my fish. I stuck it with my staff and killed it, and I was scraping the dirt off my fish when the mob began screaming and throwing things. By Lyr's barnacles, why?"

"Cats are sacred to Shekhemet. Since nobody hinders them, they take what they like."

"Why don't you kill me, then?"

Ugaph chuckled. "I have no love for the official cults. Priests magnify the powers of their gods to awe their dupes. Often I doubt if gods exist."

"Really? I knew a philosopher in Gadaira who said there were no gods or spirits, but I've known too many supernatural beings for such an extreme view."

Ugaph waved a hand. "Oh, spirits exist. In fact I, who dabble in magic, have my own familiar. But as for gods—well, there are all sorts of theories. Some say they are created by people's belief in them."

"Then let's be careful not to believe in them, lest they get power over us. But what of my fate?"

"I can use you, young man."

"For what?"

"Have you ever hunted bats?"

"No. Why should anybody hunt bats?"

"I have use for them. My daughter has been getting them for me whilst I went about my business."

"What business is that?"

"I am a collector. As I was saying, Ro has been getting my bats, but I need her help in my business. Moreover, she is likelier to catch a rich husband in the city than prowling dusty tombs."

"I see."

"And furthermore, other members of my profession sometimes try to take from me the part of these tunnels I have marked out for my own, and I need a strong arm and a keen blade to drive them out. So if you will serve as my apprentice, I will hide you, disguise you, and protect you from the superstitious mob."

"Will you also feed me and replace my garments when they wear out?"

"Surely, surely."

"Then let's begin. I was hungry when the mob drove me from my dinner, and now I'm ravenous."

Ugaph wrinkled his nose. "You are not backward. Ro, get Gezun something to eat."

The girl went into the adjoining chamber. Gezun said: "I know not how you can call collecting a business. I've heard of people who spent trade metal that way, but never of anybody who made it."

"That is simple. I am a benefactor of the people of Typhon."

"Oh?"

"You see, the temples are full of loot of which the priests have fleeced the folk by playing on their fears. I recover this stolen wealth and put it back into circulation. Like this." Ugaph showed a handful of gold, silver, and gems. The pieces of metal seemed to have been broken or cut from larger structures.

Gezun looked at the man with more respect. Of all thieves, the temple thief needed the most nerve, because of what the priests did if they caught him. The priests of Typhon, especially, were known for the ingenuity of their human sacrifices. Ro came in with a plate of food.

"Thank you, beautiful," said Gezun.

Ugaph said: "Cast no lustful eyes thither, Master

Gezun. A daughter of Setesh mates not with foreign devils. It were both immoral and unlawful. Nor think to flout me behind my back, for I have magical powers. I shall watch your every move from afar."

"So?" said Gezun, stuffing his mouth.

Next morning Gezun went to the public stables, where he had left his ass, to get his belongings. Ugaph had fitted him out to look like a Seteshan. Like other commoners of Typhon, he wore only sandals and a linen kilt. His whole head and face had been shaved, save for a short, braided scalp-lock behind and a narrow little goatee on his chin. He had left his sword and staff in the tunnels, the former because commoners were not allowed to carry them, the latter because it might help some member of yesterday's mob to recognize him.

When he had gotten back his gear and paid for fodder for his ass, Gezun rejoined Ugaph and his daughter. Ugaph said: "I will take your bags to our quarters whilst Ro shows you how to catch bats."

Gezun hesitated about giving up his bags, but Ro would serve as hostage for them. Ro carried two bags herself, one empty and the other containing food and rushlights.

"Let me bear that for you," Gezun said.

"I see your tribe of barbarians spoils its women," said Ugaph. "Farewell."

Ro led Gezun west, away from the waterfront, picking her way through the maze of crooked streets. Typhon, Gezun thought, stank even worse than Torrutseish. After an hour's walk they passed through a gate in the wall. Beyond the wall, the city thinned out to suburbs. Beyond the suburbs lay fields crisscrossed by irrigation ditches. Beyond the fields, on the skyline, lines of squat, bulky structures rose from the desert sands. Gezun had seen these on his way to Typhon.

"What are those?" he asked.

"The tombs of our kings," said Ro.

Some of the structures were true pyramids, some truncated pyramids, some stepped pyramids. The tallest of the true pyramids towered hundreds of feet high. Some were new, surrounded by complexes of walls, courts, and temples; others were old, with the complexes robbed of their stones and the pyramids themselves crumbling at the edges.

As they neared the tombs, Gezun noticed that the newer ones seemed manned. Soldiers walked the walls of the complexes, and he glimpsed priests in the courtyards.

"Who are those people?" he asked.

"The attendants of the kings of this dynasty, the ancestors of King Zeremab, on whom be life, health, and strength."

"What about the older tombs, those that seem to be falling down?"

"King Zeremab cares nought for the ghosts of kings of former dynasties. So their tombs have all been plundered and lie open to us."

"Is that where we're going?"

"Aye. I thought we should try the tomb of King Khephru. It has many passages where bats seek refuge during the day."

"Now what in the seven hells does your father want bats for?"

Ro smiled. "His familiar has a taste for bats' blood."

"You mean a familiar demon?"

"Aye, Tety. Here is Khephru's tomb."

She led him into the ruined courtyard, where the sand covered most of the pavement and half-buried such statues as remained. The original entrance to the pyramid had been blocked by blocks of granite, but spoilers had bored through the softer limestone around the granite.

"Watch your step," said Ro, leaping up the first few tiers of stone. "Are you good at making fire?"

"None better." Gezun got out his tinder box and fire stones and in a quarter-hour had a rushlight lit. Ro led him into the passage, which sloped down and forked. By the light of the rushcandle, Gezun saw more forks.

"By the beard of Roi! This place is like a rabbit warren," he said.

"Not so loud; you will frighten the bats."

They crept along, talking in whispers. Presently, Ro pointed to a little black blob on the roof of the passage. She stole up and snatched it. The bat fluttered and squeaked in her grasp, but she popped it into the bag.

"Now you try," she said.

Gezun missed his first snatch; the awakened bat whirred off into the darkness. There was a chorus of squeaks and a sense of fluttering.

"Clumsy oaf!" whispered Ro. "Now we must wait for them to quiet down again."

"A creepy place! One would expect it to be haunted."

"Some are. King Amentik's tomb has a deadly demon with wings, beak, and claws. Three men who invaded it were torn to bits."

Gezun tried for another bat and caught it. The bat bit his fingers, but its tiny teeth failed to draw blood.

In exploring one passage, they came to a place where a large block had fallen from the ceiling. Gezun trod on something hard and looked down. There were human bones on the floor, some half under the block.

"The kings put such in their tombs to foil robbers," said Ro. "When you step on a particular stone—*boom!* The ceiling falls on your head, or you fall through a trap-door. I know many such traps, some not yet sprung."

"Hm. I see your father cares not what befalls me when I go to hunt bats by myself."

"Oh, no! We do not wish you slain while you are still useful to us!"

"How kind of you!"

"Fear not; I shall tell you where to hunt each day."

After several hours' hunting the bat bag was comfortably full of squeaking, fluttering captives. It moved with a life of its own.

"That will do for today," said Ro. "Let us go back to the entrance and eat."

"I hope you know your way through this maze. Why did the kings put all these tunnels in their tombs? To mislead trespassers?"

"Partly, but also to serve as meeting places for their cults and to store their treasure, their archives, and the mummies of their kin. You'll find little treasure now, though."

At the entrance they opened the foodbag. When Gezun had eaten and drunk, he looked more closely at Ro. She was a pretty little thing. Like most women of Typhon, she wore a tight, short dress, which covered her from knee to midriff. A strip rose from the front of the dress, between her bare breasts, and encircled her neck.

Gezun ran a hand up and down her body. She slapped the hand away. "My father warned you! Tety might be watching."

Gezun let it go. There would be more opportunities.

Back in Ugaph's quarters, Ro cut the throats of the bats and bled them into a bowl, while Ugaph burned incense and chanted an incantation. When Ro had finished, there was hardly more than a big spoonful of blood in the bowl. Something appeared in the magic circle Ugaph had drawn.

At first Gezun thought it was a cat, but it was a kind of small fox with a snub nose and enormous ears. It frisked around the circle and whined. Ugaph picked up the bowl, saying:

"What news, Tety?"

The familiar spoke in a shrill bark: "The ruby in the left eye of the statue of Ip, in the temple of Ip, is loose."

"Not very helpful, as the statue is higher than a man and set back from a railing. What else?"

"The front rung in the chair of the high-priest in the temple of Neb is also loose. I think not that you can get the rung out without tools, but the golden sheathing is cracked and easily torn off . . ."

After several such responses, Tety said: "I have told you all. Now my blood!"

Ugaph put the bowl inside the circle. The beast lapped up the blood and vanished.

"What's that?" asked Gezun.

"A fennec," said Ugaph. "Now that you are an initiate bat hunter, I shall take Ro tomorrow. I will try that ruby in the temple of Ip. If she can make a disturbance—say by fainting—I'll knock the gem from its socket with that staff of yours and push it into a recess in the base of the statue. It is an ornate thing, full of hiding places. Then, after a few days, I'll slip back in and take the ruby."

"Ho!" said Gezun. "You'll not send me hunting bats by myself yet. Think you I wish to be gobbled by some demon or fall through a trapdoor?"

"Ro can tell you what to do."

"I won't do it alone."

"You shall!"

"I will not."

"I'll set the mob on you."

"Try it. They'd be interested in your little hoard of stolen sacred things."

"Well then, when will you be able to hunt by yourself?"

"It will take many days of Ro's guidance."

"He's right, father," said Ro. "If we ask too great risks from him, he'll flee."

"Oh, very well, very well. Though so far you've been of no use to me, and you eat enough for three."

Next day Ugaph, still grumbling, departed on his business, while Gezun and Ro went back to the tombs. Again Gezun made exploratory passes and was rebuffed. When he pulled her into his arms she burst into tears, babbling of her father and his demons. Gezun let her go, not because he feared Ugaph and Tety, but because he was of too kindly a nature to make the girl suffer.

So it went for a quarter-moon. Gezun made advances and accepted repulses until one day Ro began to weep almost before he started.

"What now?" he asked.

"Oh, Gezun, see you not? I am truly fond of you; it is all I can do to hold you off. When you look at me with those great brown eyes my sinews turn to water. Yet if you got me with child, my father would slay me."

"I'll take care of him."

"You talk folly. He could cut our throats any night while you lie snoring like a cataract."

"Then let's not go back to your catacombs, but flee to Kham."

"Father would charge you with felicide before the magistrate, and King Zeremab's chariots would overtake us on the road."

"Shall I cut your father's throat then?"

"Nay, not that! I should be accursed forever."

"Oh, come, you don't believe that. Your father's a sceptic."

"I know not what to believe. He cares nought for me. All he wants is for me to keep my virginity until he has sold me to a rich husband. As though one of Typhon's lords would wed the daughter of a temple thief! But I would not have him slain, especially as Tety might warn him and give him a chance to strike first."

Back in the hideaway, they found Ugaph, pale and trembly.

"It was a near thing today," he said. "A very near thing. I tried for that ruby in Ip's eye and came a hair's breadth from being caught."

"What happened?" said Gezun.

"I started to thrust with the staff at the eye when a priest came round the corner. He called me a blaspheming robber. He would have given me up to the soldiers had I not pacified him with a large offering and a tale of wishing to draw magical power from the statue. Now I must hide for a time. This priest will have warned his colleagues to watch for me."

"Let me get your supper," said Ro. "Then you'll feel better."

"It is all your fault for not having come with me. I am a poor old benefactor of humanity, but nobody gives me a chance. If there were gods, they would not let the universe run so unjustly."

All through supper, Ugaph whined about the way the world treated him. After supper, over a game of checkers with Gezun, he said:

"For once I think you foreigners are right about Setesh."

"How so?"

"They are a peevish, ungrateful lot, blindly groveling before the most cruel and gloomy gods their priests can imagine, while spurning enlighteners like me."

"Agile fellows!"

Ugaph, who seldom laughed and never saw the point of a joke, went on: "Curse of the green hippopotamus, that one of my virtue should be so put upon! And this is no life for my daughter. How shall she catch a rich husband while lurking in these crypts?"

"Why not change your ways?"

"What can I do? There is no reward for the lifter of superstition. Whoever thinks up some new and bloodthirstier divinity makes his fortune, whilst I starve in squalor—"

"Why not make our fortunes the same way?"

Ugaph stopped in mid-move, holding a draftsman. "My boy, forgive my occasional harsh words. That was a proposal of genius."

"We'll make our god the ghastliest of all. He shall hate everybody and pursue his victims unto the third and fourth generation unless propitiated by huge offerings."

"Just so! He shall demand human sacrifices, to be slain with hideous tortures."

"Why human sacrifices?"

"The Typhonians love the spectacle."

"Well," said Gezun doubtfully, "I don't mind fleecing the Typhonians, but that's going too far."

"It is a common custom here."

"So? How do you go about it?"

"One gets a license."

"But whom do you sacrifice?"

"One buys slaves or kidnaps a foreigner off the street. Nobody minds if he be not of a nation with whom the king has a treaty."

"You mean I could have been seized by some gang all the time I've been here and hauled off to a temple for carving?"

"Surely, surely. Who cares for foreign devils?"

"Well, I care for this foreign devil and will not encourage a practice that might bring my own doom. Besides, it's not a Pusadian custom. If you want my help, there shall be no more talk of that."

Ugaph argued, sulked, and gave in. Thus it came to pass that, a quarter-moon later, a peasant on the outskirts of Typhon, hoeing his plot, struck a bronze tablet.

"Praise be to Neb!" he cried as he dug it up

and brushed the dirt off. The tablet was inscribed, though he could not read. It weighed about a pound.

Two men who had been sauntering down the nearby road came over: a snaggle-toothed, middle-aged Seteshan and a gigantic young foreigner.

"What is that?" said the middle-aged one.

"I have done nought wrong, my lord," said the peasant. "I found this just now. It was on this plot, which I own in freehold, and so belongs to me."

"What will you do with it?"

"Sell it to a dealer in metals, my lord."

"Hm. Let's have a look at it."

The peasant put the tablet behind him. He could not hide it in his clothes because he wore none. "No you don't, sir. You will snatch it and run, and then where shall I be?"

"All right, you hold it and let me look at it."

Some peasants in the neighboring fields came over to see what was going on. Some travelers on the road stopped too, so presently there were a score of people around Ugaph, Gezun, and the farmer. Ugaph tilted the plaque and read loudly:

"I, Ka the Appalling, eldest and father of the gods, creator and master of the seven universes, shall soon come to dwell in Typhon in the land of Setesh. Woe to the sinners of Typhon! Now you shall be under my very eye. For, I am a great, fierce, and jealous god, at whose very name the other gods tremble. Where they beat you with switches, I shall beat you with cudgels; where they smote the sinner, I shall smite all his kin, neighbors, and friends. Repent ere it is too late! I, Ka the Omnipotent, have spoken."

Ugaph said: "This is surely a portentous matter. Fellow, I will give you half the weight of this tablet in silver, which is more trade metal than you would normally see in a lifetime. Then I shall take it into the city to see what the wise priests of Typhon make of it."

"Aye, take it!" said the peasant.

A few days later, when the rumor of the finding of the tablet had gone around, Ugaph appeared in the agora. He was naked, with red stripes on his face and ashes on his body. He foamed at the mouth (by chewing soap-wort) and altogether was the holiest-looking thing the Typhonians had seen in a long time. He waved the tablet, cried its message in a loud voice, and called on the people to repent. Gezun went about with a basket to catch the wedges and rings and bars of trade metal they tossed into it.

"A temple for Ka the Appalling!" shrieked Ugaph. "What will he think if he comes to Typhon and finds no god-house? What will he do? What will he do to us? It is our last chance . . ."

Gezun checked a smile. He composed Ugaph's speeches, since Ugaph's talents did not run that way. On the other hand, provided somebody put words in his mouth, the temple thief made a fine prophet, being of naturally solemn and pompous mien.

After another half-moon, they were counting their wealth in the hideout. Ro sorted out the different metals while Ugaph and Gezun weighed them. Ugaph, who had some small education, added up the totals on the wall of the chamber with a burnt stick. He said:

"We have more here than I have made in my whole career as a collector. Why thought I not of this before?"

"Because I wasn't here to suggest it," grinned Gezun. "Now, know you what I'd suggest further?"

"What?"

"That we put this stuff in stout bags and get out of Typhon. We could go to Kham. Your share will keep you in comfort the rest of your life, and mine will take me to all the places I have not yet seen."

"Are you mad, stripling?"

"What mean you?"

"This is nothing to what we shall collect once we get our temple built."

"You mean you would go through with that scheme and not merely talk about it?"

"Surely, surely. I have already seen Sentiu the building contractor and visited the artist Heqatari. He shall design our temple and the statue of the god."

"Then give me my half, and stay here with yours."

"No! We shall need it all. And think not to take your share by stealth. Remember, it was not I who slew the sacred cat."

Gezun glared but subsided. Ugaph might be right at that: he had more experience at this sort of thing.

Soon, the site of the temple sounded with hammering. Walls rose, floors were laid, and in the midst of it all, the great Heqatari worked with his apprentices on the statue. It was to be an imposing affair of gilded bronze, showing a vulture-headed Ka with multiple wings and arms, hurling thunderbolts and brandishing weapons.

When the workmen stopped for their noon meal, Gezun went around to where Heqatari and his apprentices gnawed bread and cheese in the shade of a wall.

"Greetings, great artist," said Gezun. "Can you explain something?"

"What?"

"What's that walled section in the rear, with the deep embayment? It was not in the original plan." Gezun pointed.

"You must mean the stable."

"Stable?"

"Aye. Ugaph has bought a chariot and pair and wishes room to store them on the temple grounds."

"Why, the foul—" began Gezun, when the clopping of hooves made him turn. There came Ugaph, standing in a gold-trimmed chariot drawn by a pair of whites. He reined up, cursing as the horses skittered and bucked and the workmen grinned at his lack of skill. Gezun strode over and began:

"What's this folly? And what mean you by commanding an enlargement of the temple without my knowledge?"

Ugaph's face darkened. "Keep your voice down, stripling, or I shall raise mine too. I might even speak of cats."

Gezun almost sprang upon Ugaph, but he mastered his rage and said: "We shall speak of this again." He walked off.

They had a furious quarrel in the underground chambers that night, Gezun pounding the table and shouting: "You profligate old fool! We're in debt far enough now to put us into debt slavery for our lives."

"And who told you how to run a cult? You think a babe like you, a third my age and a barbarian to boot, can teach me the art?"

"I can tell when an enterprise is being run to death! Instead of getting out with your paint and ashes and digging more gold out of the Typhonians, you swank around in embroidered robes and drive your gaudy toy."

"That shows your ignorance. By showing the mob how successful we are, we prove our god is truly mighty."

"Said the drunken yokel who fell down the well, how clever I am, for I shall never be thirsty! I want my share of our property, now!"

"You cannot have it. It is tied up in the temple."

"Sell my interest in it, or borrow it. But I want that trade metal."

"Impossible, you dog. When we have made our fortunes, you may ask."

"I'll go to law to force a division."

"See how far you get when the magistrate hears you are a felicide!"

Gezun started to rise, murder in his eyes, when Ro seized his arm, crying: "Gezun! Calm yourself! He has powers!"

A squeak from the corner made them turn. There sat Tety the demon in fennec-form.

"O master!" whined the fox. "It is long since you have fed me. Can I do nought for you?"

"No," said Ugaph. "Begone and bother me not."

"Pray, master! I must have bats' blood! I perish for want of the mystic ingredients."

"Begone!" yelled Ugaph, and ripped out an exorcism. The familiar vanished.

Gezun's temper had cooled, so the quarrel was dropped. For several days Ugaph worked at his evangelism, crying doom about the agora while Gezun collected. Gezun noted that the collections were dwindling.

"By Neb's toenails, it will soon not be worth while," grumbled Ugaph one evening. "All the Typhonians have heard our message and await something new. We must hurry the temple."

"How long will it take?" said Gezun. "By Sentiu's original promises it should be done, but the roof is not yet up."

"That is the way with builders. I see where we made several mistakes, but when we build our big temple those shall be corrected."

"What big temple?"

"Oh, this is only a small affair. As our cult grows, this building will not hold our congregation. We shall build a magnificent structure, like the temple of Shekhemet."

"Hmp. You mean, after you've paid off my share."

"Why so eager to withdraw?"

"I tire of Typhon. They hate foreigners as one would expect of some backward Atlantean village, but not of a great city. Besides, it is too hot, and the fleas and flies give one no peace."

Ugaph shrugged. "Each to his taste. Tomorrow I will oversee the putting up of the roof."

Next morning, after Ugaph left, Gezun was loafing and watching Ro clean up their breakfast, when Tety appeared, whining: "Good foreign devil, my master neglects and spurns me. I starve for bats' blood."

"That's sad, little one," said Gezun.

"Can you do nought for me?"

Gezun started to say no, then grinned and said to Ro: "Beautiful, those bat hunts were fun. Let's make another."

"But that long walk? In this heat?"

"We'll use the chariot. It's half mine. And the tombs are cool."

"Oh, bless you, dear mortal!" said Tety.

Hours later they were deep in the bowels of King Khephru's pyramid. When their game bag was full they went to the entrance and ate. Then Gezun pulled Ro to him and kissed her. She resisted, but not enough, so that what started as a youthful game turned into a real love tussle.

A little later, Gezun slept in the tunnel entrance, snoring thunderously, while Ro wept for her lost maidenhood and covered his face with damp kisses.

Ugaph hung around the temple until Heqatari flew into a tantrum. He cursed Ugaph and all his ancestors, because, he said, Ugaph got in his way, distracted him by idiotic suggestions, and did not understand that the artistic soul was purer and finer than the souls of common men.

Ugaph, disgruntled, went to the stable where he kept his chariot. He was even more vexed to learn that his partner had taken the vehicle. Scowling, he walked to the palace and gained admittance to the office of the Registrar of Licenses. He asked for a license for human sacrifice.

"You know the rules?" said the Registrar.

"Surely, surely, my lord. Pusadians are not among the protected groups of foreigners, are they?"

"What are Pusadians?"

"Far-western barbarians. Is everything in order, then?"

"The priests of Neb and Shekhemet and the others are up in arms over your competition, but we cannot afford to offend any god. So here is your license."

"I abase myself in humble gratitude, my lord. Come to one of our services."

Ugaph backed out, bowing. Next he went to the thieves' quarter, a tumbledown part of the city where people were either too poor to escape or sought refuge there from King Zeremab's soldiers and officials. He sought out a brawny cutthroat named Eha, whom he had known in his thieving days. He said:

"Are you looking for work, old comrade?"

Eha grinned and flexed a muscle. "I might, if it meant enough metal and not too much work."

"I need a couple of stout fellows to help me with the temple: to sweep the floor, guard the loot, and the like. Have you a friend I could trust?"

"What about that foreign devil, your partner?"

"I think we shall not long be troubled with him. Are you up to desperate deeds?"

"You know me, Ugaph."

Eha got his friend, a silent hulk named Maatab. Ugaph took them to the temple and put them to work on small tasks, such as moving the gear from the hideaway to the temple when the dwelling rooms were finished. Gezun made only a mild objection to hiring this pair, as Ugaph explained that three could not do all the work of the cult. Gezun was going about starry-eyed, as he had decided he was in love again. Ugaph, who might have been expected to notice the signs that Gezun and Ro gave of their attachment, seemed to pay no attention.

The day came when the last bit of plaster had dried, the last mural had been painted, and the last patch of gold leaf had been hammered into place. Ugaph called Gezun, Ro, Maatab, and Eha into conference. He sat at the head of the table in a gold-embroidered robe of shiny eastern stuff and a tall, pointed hat. He said:

"Tomorrow night is our dedication. The temple will be filled. I have bought an ox for sacrifice to get things started. But our future depends on this ceremony's going smoothly, to get our pious fools worked up to a big donation. Let us be sure we all know our parts perfectly . . ."

When they had rehearsed again, Ugaph said: "Gezun, Maatab and Eha and I are going to fetch our ox. I leave you here to guard the temple. We shall be gone an hour."

He led the two thieves out. Gezun looked at Ro. He had not been alone with her for any length of time since that day in Khephru's tomb. All that made him hesitate was that Ugaph's parting words sounded almost like an invitation. But for one of Gezun's age and vigor, the contest between lust and suspicion was too one-sided to last long.

Ugaph led Maatab and Eha to the main chamber of the temple. In front of the statue of Ka, Ugaph said: "How is your courage?"

Maatab laughed and Eha made muscles.

"Good," murmured Ugaph. "The plan I have discussed is the one that young dog thinks we shall follow. But what we shall really do is this: He will be in his room at the beginning of the service, primping. He will come out thinking he is to enter the main chamber and slay the ox with the sanctified ax. But you two—"

Eha broke in: "Is it wise to talk of this so near the god?" He jerked his head towards the brooding idol.

"Ha! That is but a thing of bronze and wood. I planned it and Heqatari made it, just as I invented Ka and his whole cult. Unless we believe in a god, he cannot exist." Ugaph spat at the statue. "If you fear . . ."

"I? Fear?" protested both thieves at once.

"Well then, listen. As Gezun steps from his room, you two shall seize him. Slay him not, nor even stun him deeply. I wish him awake during the sacrifice; the throng loves the screams of the victim. Bind his wrists and ankles firmly and bear him to the main chamber. Lay him on the altar, and I shall do the rest . . ."

In his chamber, Gezun could hear the voices of the congregation as Ugaph led them in a hymn, for which Ro played a lyre. He put the last touches on his costume: a knee-length kilt embroidered with gold thread, gilded sandals, and an ornate conical cap like Ugaph's but not so tall. He listened for his cue. When it came, he stepped to the doorway. His hand was out to thrust the curtain aside when he heard a squeak. There was Tety.

"Gezun!" said the familiar.

"What is it?"

"There is something you must know—"

"No time! Tell me after the service." Gezun reached for the curtain again.

"It is a matter of life and death."

"By the holy crocodile of Haides! Eha and Maatab will be leading in the ox. Save it till later."

"But it is your death! They will slay you instead of the ox."

Gezun stopped. "What's this?"

Tety told of Ugaph's orders. "I was hovering in my

spirit form in the temple and came to warn you because of that bats' blood."

"But why should Ugaph slay me?"

"To get sole ownership, to give the Typhonians a gory show, and to see that you shall not object to such sacrifices in the future."

Gezun saw he had been a fool. With a smothered curse he leaped for his belongings and got out the double-curved Tartessian sword. "We shall see who sacrifices whom!"

"Go not into the main chamber!"

"Why not?"

"I know not, but there are portentous stirrings on the spiritual plane. Something dreadful will happen."

"Hm. Anyway, my thanks, little devil."

Gezun went to the doorway on tiptoe. He stood to one side of the door and jerked the curtain aside. Seeing movement in the dark corridor, he snatched and caught a muscular arm. With a mighty heave, he pulled Eha into the room. Eha struck at him with a short, leaden bludgeon.

As Eha was off-balance at the time, the blow did not hit squarely. It knocked off Gezun's wizard's hat and grazed his shaven scalp, filling his eyes with stars. He thrust the sword into Eha's neck.

Eha stumbled to hands and knees with a gurgle, dropping the club. Maatab bounded into the room. Gezun tried to withdraw the sword from Eha, but it stuck fast. Then Maatab was upon him.

They staggered back into the middle of the room, kicking, punching, gouging, and grabbing for holds. Maatab hooked a thumb into Gezun's nostrils, but Gezun kicked Maatab in the crotch and sent the Seteshan back groaning. They clinched, fell, and rolled. Gezun felt the bludgeon under his hand. He picked it up and struck at

Maatab. The blow struck Maatab's shoulder. Maatab broke away and tore the sword out of Eha.

Then they were up again, feinting, dodging, and striking. Each leaped at the other for a finishing blow, but each caught the other's wrist. They staggered about, each trying to wrench his right arm out of the other's grasp. Gezun felt a grip on his ankle. It was Eha, not yet dead. Gezun fell heavily. Maatab leaped for him, but Gezun flung up both legs and drove his heels into Maatab's belly. The Seteshan was flung back against the wall. He dropped the sword and half fell, coughing and gasping.

Gezun rose and lunged for the sword. There was an instant of floundering as each tried to pick up the weapon and at the same time to kick aside or stamp on the other's groping hand. Then Gezun kicked the sword out into the middle of the room. He scooped it up and straightened to slash at Maatab, who turned and half fell out the doorway.

To kill time, Ugaph had stretched his sermon, reiterating the awfulness, ferocity, and vindictiveness of Ka the Appalling. Then, instead of a bound Gezun being carried out by Eha and Maatab, Maatab appeared running with Gezun after him. Maatab stumbled around to the front of the statue, trying to cry a warning but too winded to speak. Both were disheveled, their kilts torn, their faces and bodies covered by bruises and scratches. Sweat and blood ran down their limbs. Ro dropped her lyre with a twang.

"He—he—" gasped Maatab, dodging behind Ugaph.

"I'll—" panted Gezun.

Ugaph retreated towards the crowd, shrieking: "Seize the felicide! He is the foreign devil who slew the cat in the Month of the Camel! Tear him to pieces!"

A murmur in the congregation rose to a roar. Much as Gezun wanted to see the blood of Ugaph and Maatab spurt, he did not wish to be torn to bits afterwards. The crowd fell silent. He stepped back towards the statue and glanced at Ro.

Ro was staring at a point behind him and some feet over his head. He looked up. An arm of gilded bronze, ending in a clawed hand like the foot of a bird of prey, was coming down upon him.

Gezun made a tremendous leap. The wind of the snatch fanned his back.

With a loud creaking, the statue stepped heavily down from its dais. Ugaph and Maatab stared in unbelieving horror, while behind them the audience began to scream and stampede. Ugaph and Maatab turned to run, but two long arms shot out. One arm seized each man, the claws sinking deeply. Ka raised the two kicking, screaming men towards his vulture's beak.

Gezun caught Ro's wrist and dragged her through the other door. Back in the corridor, he started for the door to the stable. Then he said: "Wait! Hold this!"

"But Gezun—"

He pressed his sword into her hands and darted into Ugaph's chamber. On the floor lay the chest containing their liquid funds. It was locked and chained to a ring in the wall. Gezun picked up the chest and gave it a mighty heave as if to throw it. On the first try the chain held, but on the second the staple pulled out of the wall. Gezun ran out with the chest under one arm.

The screams from the main chamber of the temple came higher and higher. They faded behind Gezun as he pulled Ro out to the stable, hitched up the whites, whirled the chariot around, and set out for the north gate at a gallop. They skidded around turns.

"What—what happened?" said Ro.

"Your father didn't believe in Ka, but he convinced so many others that their belief called the god to life."

"But why did Ka animate the statue and attack Father?"

"Well, he was described as fierce and vindictive, so he'd

be angry when I wasn't sacrificed as promised. Or perhaps he resented Ugaph's atheism." He slowed the team to a trot. "Let's stop at the fountain to make ourselves look respectable, or the guards won't let us out of the gate."

A few minutes later, Gezun whipped up the whites and galloped out on the long level desert road to Kham in the land of Kheru. Behind him, a somber shadow seemed to brood over Typhon.

"Anyway," he said, "I'm through with experiments having to do with gods. Men are hard enough to deal with."

LATEST
Science
Fiction!

e. e. "doc" smith
A master of ★★★★ science fiction